I0583110

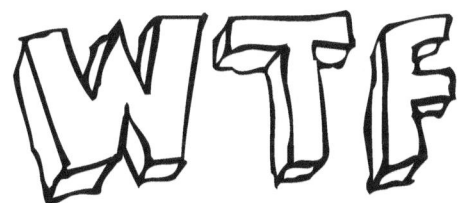

WTF

Scarlett J Rose.

Dedicated to My partner-in-crime, and in life.

Steve. ♥

With special kick-arse thanks to:

Susan Horsnell, Joanne Effendi, Cheryl Riddell, Helen King

And you, my readers! For without you, there'd be no book to be read!

WTF © 2018 Scarlett J Rose

This book is a work of fiction. Any resemblance to people, places, or events is unintentional and coincidental.

All Rights Reserved.

This book is protected by international copyright.

If you have seen or downloaded this book using a pirating site, please note that this is illegal, and hurts the author more than you can ever know. I would ask that you contact the publisher/author to inform them of the illegal copies so appropriate action may be taken.

Edited by: Joanne Effendi

Cover by SJR Covers using images purchased on Depositphotos.com

ISBN: 978-0-6480098-6-3

Follow Scarlett J Rose on Facebook:
www.facebook.com/scarlettjrose/

Paperback Versions of this book are available through Scarlett's Facebook Page, please send a message if you'd like to order one – I'll even happily sign it!

Other books by Scarlett J Rose:

Independent books:

The FML Series:

FML

WTF

OMG *(Coming soon!)*

Redemption of the Fallen Series.

Demon's Embrace

Angel's Redemption

Demon's Bargain (*Coming Soon!*)

Maelstrom MC.

Firestorm.

Broken Flowers:

Desert Rose

Evernight Publishing:

The Trenin Alliance:

Subject 26-A

(2017 Evernight Publishing Reader's choice runner up in Science-fiction Category)

Fallen Star

Romance on the Go Standalones.

Guarding Her

The Indecent Proposal of Mrs Cortez

More to come!

'Like' Scarlett J Rose on Facebook for upcoming releases and more information!

www.facebook.com/scarlettjrose/

Chapter One.

"Gorgeous"

Click.

"Just lean against him a little."

Click.

"Okay, one more in that position."

Click.

"Great! Now the mums and dads, if you can come and join the bride and groom?"

I looked up from prepping the Polaroid camera for my boss Danny, as the families of the happy couple joined the bride and groom for their photograph. Danny was in his element, but I wanted a little more from my life than just taking photos and happy snaps of happy families.

It was all a fucking illusion; my shitty childhood had taught me that. I knew there were people out there who were happy. Two such examples were my best friend, Mel and her husband, movie star Adam Jacobs, and Mel's parents, who owned the nursery and gardens we were shooting the wedding photos in.

My own romantic endeavours basically revolved around Friday night hook-ups and the subsequent 'Walk of Shame'—or in my case the stagger of shame—early on a Saturday morning.

Danny reached out behind him for the Polaroid camera. I quickly handed it to him, grabbing the digital camera he'd used, and connected it to the work laptop to upload and backup. I looked over the gorgeous pictures, knowing that Danny had an eye for detail, one he'd said countless times that I possessed, despite my obnoxious scoffing.

Okay, so I had an eye for when the lighting was just right, juxtaposition of things, took some great action shots, and my prints had sold well to the tourists when we had the local craft market.

But I wanted more. To *be* more. To learn more. To become kick-arse and awesome. Yeah, I was a lil' spitfire, who went on weekly benders up the local pub, had a bigger-than-life attitude and flipped the bird at life if it pissed me off. This shit was normal to me. Nothing in life was easy, I knew that, but I didn't want it to be so fucking hard that I was going to be forced to live a life of mediocracy in a place where I was conceived, born and dragged up.

A place where my grandparents and parents couldn't get out of…well Dad got out, if you call dying in prison getting out. And my mum? She checked out years ago, dotty as fuck, decades of alcohol abuse rotting her brain until she overdosed at one of her boyfriend's places. I knew if I wasn't careful, I'd end up just like her and the old man. My 'lovely' parents were one of the reasons why I only bended on Fridays.

I heard my phone's message notification go off. While the camera uploaded the shots to the laptop, I checked the phone. Mel had messaged me, letting me know she was back home. I was headed to her place after this shoot to get ready for a date later that night. I'd been going around with this bloke for about three weeks. So far, so good. Shagging him was pretty fucking awesome. He had a few special 'tricks' that I hadn't had anyone else try before. He told me he had something special planned for tonight, and if my pink bits weren't excited, then I wasn't a red-blooded woman.

Some might call me a slapper, or a tart, skank, ho-bag—all those lovely names for a lass who just wants to have a bit of fun with a bloke. Yeah, blokes are players, women are sluts. Hooray for equal fucking opportunity! Honestly, I didn't give a shit what anyone thought. I lived it hard when I was a kid. I deserve a bit of fun. And if anything happens? I deal with it, like an adult, or I kick them in their bits. Either way works fine.

I smirked, Mel wanted me to swing by early if I could. She was having issues dealing with being 'fatter than a bloody whale', otherwise known as so preggers she was almost ready to pop. Her firstborn was due in a month, or just under, and Adam was away shooting some multi-bazillion dollar chick flick that would have some crazy stalker bitches after his very sexy body. Yes, I look, but I do not touch. That's a big fat fucking deal breaker. I'm not going to be labelled a homewrecker or a cheater.

I texted my bitch back, telling her I'd be there ASAP, with her choice of sweeties, as well as a box of chips n' gravy from the cafe in the village. It would mean a quick trip into the village, instead of heading up the small drive beside her parent's cottage to the gorgeous house that Adam had built for their main home here in the UK, but hell, Mel was my best friend, and had been there for me for so much of the shitty parts of my childhood. We were practically sisters.

With my pre-date plans set, I finished the upload to the laptop while Danny finished with the polaroid as the wedding party moved back towards the vintage Rolls Royce cars they'd used for the wedding.

We packed everything away. Danny would be continuing his photographer duties at the reception. I'd been given the rest of the night off, which was lucky, because I'd already told him I had plans, and thankfully, Danny was an accommodating boss.

I loaded my own cameras and gear into my trusty little car and jumped in. As soon as I turned the key, the *Dead Sinners Society* pounded their fucking-awesomely-kick-arse Death Metal through my skull via my speakers. Yours truly had been most fortunate and honoured to have been the meat in the sandwich with Lars and Jorgen, lead singer and drummer from the DSS. And damn, if it weren't one fucking awesome one-night stand. I still have very, *very* fond memories of that epic night... It was also the night that Mel reunited with her true love, Adam... Yeah sappy shit, but hey, she's happy and that's what matters.

I drove down the country roads, swerving around farmers in slow-moving tractors until I came to the village centre. Lisa Cunningham, one of the local coppers was waiting in the chip shop for her order. She grinned at me when I stepped up next to her after placing my order.

"Hey Lis." I grinned, she'd also gone to high school with Mel and me. She was considered one of the really geeky kids back then. Who knew, that years of being called names because of her braces and glasses, would drive her to become a cop? And one heck of a cop too. This chick was fearless.

"Hey Libby, how was that wedding you were shooting at?" she asked with a grin.

"I give 'em six months, tops. The groom was too busy checking out the maid-of-honour's tits in the low-cut gown she wore, to notice than his own bride was giving him death glares."

"Ha! That'll teach him. Bloody men, eh? Ya can't live with 'em, can't bury em in the backyard, eh?" Lisa grinned.

I chuckled with her. "That's the truth there."

"Yeah, well, unfortunately, I'm showing a new bloke the ropes today. Comes from London. Poor bastard is gonna die of boredom here."

"Well, this isn't the most exciting place. I mean we do have our little break-ins here and there, usually the kids from the village getting into the whisky. But nothing too bad." I grinned.

"Yeah, poor bugger probably just wants a nice holiday from the shite going down in London these days. Be nice for him to have a normal life for a bit I think."

"Define 'normal' these days?" I snorted.

"Good point." Lis chuckled. She reached over to the drinks fridge and cracked open a bottle of cola. "How's our favourite superstar wife these days?"

"Beautiful, and about ready to pop too, I think. Maybe another couple of weeks, but this is her first, so anything goes." I didn't like to gossip too much about Mel's life. People wanted the ins and outs and minute details, when really, they should be looking inwards on their own pathetic excuse, not living vicariously through someone else.

"Well, let her know we're all thinking of her," Lis said as my order was called.

"Will do." I grabbed the butcher-paper-wrapped parcel of greasy chips and the plastic container of gravy and headed out to my car... Where a cop was writing out a ticket and slapping it on my front windshield.

"What the fuck?!"

Chapter Two.

Okay, so apart from being royally pissed that some arsehole cop was writing me out a ticket for being a SINGLE FUCKING INCH over the parking line…claiming I was 'double parked', this guy was hot… And not just hot, but, fuck me, he was so fucking hot I swear my knickers just spontaneously combusted, leaving me with third degree burns all over my pink bits.

"What the fuck are you doing?" I asked him as I stormed up to my car, my package of chips tucked up under my arm. "You seriously gonna give me a ticket for being a teeny bit over the line? What are you, some kind of fucking parking Nazi or something?" I could feel my blood boiling. I never got a ticket in this town, I drank with the local coppers regularly on a Friday night, I'd even shagged constable Lee Donahue a couple of times. I was good with the local cops.

"Libby? Everything all right? Oh, I see you've met Senior Constable Richard Handcock." Lisa gestured to me. "Richard, this is Elizabeth Hastings, one of the local photographers."

"Nice to meet you, Dick." I said with a sneer as I shoved the offending ticket in my bag.

"Richard." He corrected me as I opened the car door and slid into the driver's seat and shut the door.

"Yeah, but you'll always be 'Dick' to me." I smarted off as I turned the key in the ignition and let the bass drown out anything else the tosser might have said.

I pulled out, almost colliding with Mrs Tompkins, who really shouldn't have her licence at her age. Poor old bat could barely see over the steering wheel, and her glasses were so thick, you could use them as astral telescope lenses.

"Fucking cocksucker, I mean, seriously, a ticket for not even an inch over! That wanker won't last five minutes in this town." I griped to myself as the soothing pounding base and sexy, raspy voice of Lars thumped through my head.

I left the village, heading back to the nursery and gardens, behind which Mel lived. She had taken over the business with her brother, providing florists with beautiful blooms, and backyard gardeners with all their plant needs. She'd been living in LA with Zane, a gay friend of hers, until her father had a severe stroke.

Poor Mr Whittaker was going to be wheelchair bound for the rest of his life, and still had a bit of a stutter, but he was always in the workshops, helping to set up florists' orders or slowly wheeling himself through the gardens that Mel herself had designed, complete with a hedge maze and playground for the kids who visited with their parents.

I turned off the road, just before the nursery drive, and in to Mel's parent's property. They had a small road that led behind their cottage and back down to Mel's property.

I typed in the security code at Mel's gate and waved at the camera. Adam had a bit of security here, mainly to keep their privacy, something I could completely understand. I mean, when you're married to one of the hottest, most fucking sought-after movie stars on the planet, then, yeah, I'd want security too.

I pulled up in one of the parking spots, right next to Mel's car, a new model Range Rover. One she never really drove, unless she absolutely had to… Mel was an absolutely woeful driver. She was so bad, that Adam had hired her a driver for her birthday, whom she hardly used.

I got out of my car and headed up to the front door. Before I could reach the handle, it opened, and Zane stood there with a smirk on his face.

"Hey Slag." He grinned, his American twang making the word sound strange.

"What are you doing here, Fag? I thought you'd be cruising for the local 'talent'." I chuckled, knowing he wouldn't take offence to the word. Since Robbie and I contacted Zane to organise a surprise visit for Mel's birthday two years ago, we'd become pretty chummy. I had become one of his coveted 'Fag-Slags', along with Mel, and another of her friends back in the states called Fiona.

"Oh, you know, tending to 'Madam Whale'." He sniggered.

"Hey! I heard that!" Mel's voice called out from the entry.

"Oops," Zane said with a wry grin.

I shook my head. "You'll learn one day, my lad, that teasing a heavily pregnant woman will get you squashed." I smiled at Zane, hoping I came across as wise and knowledgeable.

"Hey Slapper, how are you feeling?" I asked Mel.

"Like a bloody beached whale," she said, placing her hands at the small of her back. "I swear if I start laughing I'm going to wet my pants." She looked at Zane and then me, her face serious. "So, no larks, got it?"

"Got it!" Zane said, placing his hands up in a surrendering gesture. Mel smiled and turned, waddling back inside the house. "She's testy today," Zane stage whispered.

"I heard that!" Mel shouted back.

I entered the beautiful home of my best friend. Zane took the bag holding my little black dress from me as I passed him.

"Ooh…pretties!" He squealed like a teenaged girl who had come across her superstar crush all alone in a parking lot.

"Take care of that, it's my most prized possession…after my cameras. Cost me a fucking arm and a leg, and most of my lady bits too."

"That's okay sweetheart, I won't harm your *precious.*" Zane imitated Gollum from *The Lord of the Rings*.

"That right there, is creepy as fuck." I shook my head as we walked up the stairs to the guest rooms where Mel had already run me a bath.

"Did he do Gollum?" Mel asked, poking her head out of the guest room door where we were headed.

"Yes! This guy is seriously freaky, where did you find him again?" I asked her as I entered the room. The scent of rose and lavender bath oils drifted through from the ensuite bathroom.

"Los Angeles," Mel said, lowering herself on to the bed with a sigh.

"Oh, weren't those some decadent times?" Zane giggled. Mel smiled and flipped him the bird.

"Everything is your fault, you know." She grinned.

"Yes, yes, It's my fault you're in this condition." Zane leaned down and gave Mel a chaste kiss on the temple. "But it's not all about me tonight, tonight…" He spun around dramatically and faced me. "It's all about Miss Libby here." He grinned wickedly. "She's going to get good and fucked."

"I think the term you're looking for, Zane is: 'shagged rotten.'" Mel supplied.

"Abso-fucking-loutly." I agreed.

"Right, get your ass in that bath bitch," Zane said, giving me a friendly push towards the bathroom.

By the time I'd finished, my body shone with bath oils, I was wearing a light, but expensive perfume, courtesy of Mel, and my little black dress had been accessorised to the nines by Zane, who had gone from movie extra, to phone sex operator, to webcam model, to drag queen and was now between professions. The drag queen dream had ended spectacularly thanks to Mel, during what was now deemed 'DragGate'. Two years ago, on Mel's birthday, we had surprised her by taking her to a Drag Queen show that Zane was debuting in and had been touring around the UK from America. Mel, in one of her famous clumsy moments had accidentally tripped over on stage, where she was being serenaded by the Drag Queens for her birthday, and had caused some seriously major wardrobe malfunctions for the two drag queens on either side of her.

There were plastic titties everywhere.

Zane had dubbed it a tit-tastrophe, and the Drag Queens had refused to speak with him ever again, except for their friend, Perry, or Miss Periwinkle, who was aware of Mel's infamous two left feet.

I left Mel and Zane, who were going to have a girl's night in, due to Mel's condition, and watch bad romantic movies all night long with popcorn.

In hindsight, I probably should have joined them instead of going to my date.

I found him sitting at our table, with another woman. Whom he introduced as his wife, and introduced me as his girlfriend *to* his wife.

Then, the pillock proceeded to invite me to a threesome with said wife.

"What the Fuck?"

Chapter Three.

I looked at my 'date' and his wife.

"Are you fucking kidding me right now?" I asked, my voice rising. "You're fucking *married?*"

"Come now, Elizabeth, don't cause a scene, dear. Let's all sit down and discuss this like adults, we can have a lot of fun together." He had the audacity to smile at me.

"My name...you fucking arsehole, is *Libby*. I don't fuck married men, and I ain't into bitches." I grabbed the glass of water that sat innocently on the table and tossed it in his face before I stormed out of the ritzy restaurant.

I was so fucking angry with that tosser.

How dare he think that I wanted to fuck him *and* his wife? How the fuck did I miss that he was married? I went through it all in my mind as I got in my car. The signs were there. But I didn't read them right. The phone call he'd had on our first date that he'd had to take outside, the slight lightness of skin on his ring finger and the way he kept saying I was 'perfect'. I grumbled under my breath as I unlocked my car door and slid inside, slamming it shut.

I didn't need this shite. I could have been helping Danny at work, instead of chasing a dick for a good time. I started the car, the noise of *DSS* pounding through my car and body. It looked like it was going to be a 'good vibrations' kinda night with Handy Andy, my vibrator. He would do in a pinch, or when desperation got the better of me.

I lit up a cigarette and inhaled the acrid smoke, enjoying the burn in my lungs. I'd been good around Mel, never smoking around her, and not because she asked me to, but because I knew she was going to be a worry-wort all through the pregnancy and I didn't want my best friend stressing any more than I knew she would.

Pulling out of my parking spot, I drove down towards the main street of the village. Anger at the arsehole burning in my gut. I slowed briefly at a stop sign before I rolled on through, making sure there were no other cars coming. I accelerated through the streets, but the tell-tale flashing blue and red lights blazed through the night, illuminating my little car's interior.

"Great, just fucking great." I grumbled around the cigarette as I pulled over and parked my car out of the way. I wound the window down, letting the heavy bass pound through the quiet streets, setting the neighbourhood dogs barking and howling. Lights started to come on in the dark houses along the street. I looked in the mirror and watched as the flashing lights caught the figure of the copper as they came up to my window.

"Good evening Miss. Can you turn down the stereo please?" A male voice asked just loud enough to be heard over the falsetto screaming of Lars.

"Sorry, can't. Knob's broken," I shouted, taking a drag on my cigarette. I blew a smoke ring. A thick arm reached in and turned the ignition off. I glimpsed a tattoo of a girl's name *'Daisy'* surrounded in the white flowers of her namesake, in the shape of a heart on the hairy forearm of the officer. The noise of my stereo died with the engine as the officer took my keys.

"Hey! I need those back!"

"Step out of the car, please, Miss." The voice seemed familiar. I looked up at the copper as I got out of the car, stumbling a little on the old cobblestone road in my high heels.

"Well, Constable Dick." I grinned, pronouncing 'constable' as '*cunt-stable*'. "We meet again."

He eyed me with an eyebrow raised at the obvious insult, but said nothing about it. "Licence please," he said, holding out his ticket book and scribbling in it.

"Sure. It's in my car," I said, turning around and leaning back into my car. Again, stumbling on the damp cobbles in my heels.

I reached in and grabbed my handbag, backing up a little too quickly, and felt my ass connect with him. His hands gripped my hips, fingers digging into the flesh as well as something else.

"That's not what you think it is." Came the strained voice behind me.

"That better be your taser," I said straightening slowly, as I moved a step forward.

"It is," he assured me, taking my proffered licence. "Ah, yes Miss Hastings, I do remember you now. Got that parking ticket sorted yet?"

I gave him a deadpan glare.

"Have you had any alcohol this evening? You seem a little unsteady on your feet."

"Nope, no alcohol, though the night is young." I huffed, hoping this wouldn't take long.

"You know what a stop sign is?" he asked, writing down my details in the ticket book.

"Yes, I know what a fucking stop sign is." I grumped.

"Good, then you'll know the reason I'm giving you a ticket then." He smirked, ripping the ticket out of the book and handing it to me.

"You're fucking kidding me right now?" I sighed, and ran my free hand over my face, before putting the cigarette back to my lips and reading over the ticket.

"Have a nice evening miss, and get home safely. Oh, and remember the road rules, or you'll be seeing a lot more of me."

"Oh, I'm sure I will…*cunt*-stable Dick," I muttered as he walked back to his car and jumped in, he pulled up beside me as I got into the driver's side of my own.

"And Miss Hastings? You'd better get your stereo fixed, or you might end up getting pulled over again for noise pollution laws."

I snorted as he drove off and went to turn on my car—but the bastard had taken my fucking keys!

"What the fuck!"

Chapter Four.

I got out of my car and watched as his tail lights turned a corner.

"Fuck, fuck, fuck, fuck, fuck!" I shouted, stamping my heeled foot for emphases. It fucking turned on the cobblestones, my ankle twisting painfully as I went down like a sack of shite.

I huffed a lock of hair out of my face as the heavens opened and fat, cold drops of rain began to fall. "Fuck," I grumbled as a got up and locked up the car.

Moments later, I was hobbling along the wet footpath, each step agony to my swelling ankle. Alcohol was certainly called for. I hobbled to the nearest pub with full intentions of getting good and stonkered. I'd have to come to the police station tomorrow to pick up my keys once I was sober enough, but fuck it, after tonight's disastrous date and the thieving copper stealing my keys, I needed a shot of vodka…followed by a pint of lager, then a few more shots of something. I got all that, but after the last few shots, it got a little blurry.

I remember having a couple of guys try to pick me up, and even one or two women who eyed my cleavage with hot looks, but I stand by my principles, and sexuality choices…not that I haven't experimented a little bit in community college. I didn't find myself attracted to my own gender like some of the other girls. I like dick, not pussy. I don't judge others if they do like their own flavours, but I'm a happy hetero.

The pub was getting rowdy by my seventh drink. The place was a bit wobbly, and I didn't feel the pain from my ankle, which was fucking fantastic.

"Fuck you all, cocksuckers and motherfuckers!" I cheered, standing on the bar, raising my vodka shot to the bar patrons.

"Okay, I think you've had enough. Get off the bar, miss," the bartender ordered me.

"Nope! I'm queen of the fucking pub! These, these are my people!" I slurred.

"Miss, you need to get down or I'm going to have you removed." The bar keeper commanded me again.

"You don't tell me what to fucking do…" I slurred. There seemed to be another bartender, who looked exactly the same as the first…but slightly to the left and a bit blurred.

The doors to the pub opened as the bartender tried to get me down again.

"That's okay, I've got her." I peered through the alcohol haze at the blurry blob that approached my perch. I was swept off my feet and carried out of the pub.

"Robbie?" I was surprised that Mel's brother had come into the pub.

"Yes, it's me, your prince charming, come to rescue you."

"But, I can't fucking leave yet! They have to hear my royal speech!" I cried… Somehow it was really important that the patrons of the pub heard my speech. "I'm the queen of the pub!"

"Sorry, your majesty, but you've been cut off, and you're lucky I was swinging in for a pint with a friend and saw you. What the hell are you doing here anyway? Weren't you on a date?"

"The bastard is fucking married," I bemoaned as Robbie set me down.

I squealed as pain shot up my ankle, I lifted the offended leg and held it, hopping unsteadily on the good foot.

"Shit, Libby, what happened?"

I couldn't help it, but started to babble as he helped me to the van. The diatribe of drunken words tumbled from my alcohol-numbed lips.

"Robbie, why can't I find a nice guy?" I said, the alcohol doing its work and bringing me down from my drunken high.

"I don't know, love," he replied, kneeling in front of me. "But let's get you home, get some ice on that ankle, and get you out of that damp dress and into something warm. Where are your keys?"

"*Cuntstable* Dick took them," I said, leaning against the back of the passenger seat as Robbie eased the shoe off my injured foot.

"Who is '*Cuntstable* Dick'?" Robbie asked me with a frown.

I hiccupped before I felt my stomach rebel a little. "He's an arsehole," I mumbled against the headrest of the passenger seat.

I was sleepy. Robbie tossed the shoe he'd removed from my foot into the van and reached over me, pulling the seatbelt across and clipping it in. I was dozing by the time he'd gotten into the driver's seat and started the drive out of the village and back to the Whittaker's place.

I vaguely remembered him pulling up at the front door of Mel's place, and carrying me up the steps and to one of the guest rooms. The bed was like a fluffy cloud of awesomeness and I crashed out into the drunken world of nod.

I woke up with a pounding head and a desperate need to puke. I opened my eyes and looked around, desperate to find where I was, and the location of the nearest loo. I recognised the room as one of Mel's guest rooms. As soon as my feet touched the floor, I fell down, one ankle swollen and throbbing with pain as I cried out, trying to hold back the wave of nausea that threatened to embarrass me.

I crawled on hands and knees to the bathroom, barely making it in time to lift the lid and seat of the toilet and evacuate the contents of my sour stomach into the blue chemical treated water of the toilet.

"Ahh… Our queen is awake!" Robbie chuckled from behind me as I felt a cool, damp cloth pressing over the back of my neck. "Good thing you've got a pixie style cut, Libby." I moaned in response and lifted a middle finger in salute to him. The fucker laughed.

"Sorry love, your pain is self-inflicted. You'll get no sympathy from me." He sighed, as I heaved again. "So, I'm heading into town soon on the afternoon delivery runs, if you want to get your keys from the police station. I've called already, and they have them waiting for you to pick up. Someone named Constable Handcock said he'd meet you when you came in."

"*Cuntstable* Dick…" I groaned and heaved again. Surely my stomach was empty by now!

"Oh dear, our sleeping beauty has awoken." Zane's American twang hit my pounding head.

"Fuck off, I'm dying here." I moaned.

"Yes, I can see that. Oh Libby, you are just like our Mel, before she got in the family way."

"Taught her everything I knew." I groaned, reaching to the back of my neck and pulling the damp washcloth over my face. I wiped my mouth, ignoring the putrid stink of undigested alcohol and vomit. "Now, gentlemen, if you'll excuse me, I need to take a shower. Zane, can you grab my emergency clothes from the bag in Mel's wardrobe?"

"Ah, you mean the 'Libby got drunk and crashed at Mel's place' bag?" He smirked.

"That'd be the one." I nodded, then groaned as another pulse of pain throbbed through my head. "Okay, evacuate the bathroom…" I groaned as I pushed myself up from the temple of the porcelain gods and flushed my offering. Robbie smiled and turned the water on in the shower for me before he left. Zane had already left to retrieve my emergency clothing. I stripped and stepped under the warm stream of water, letting it pulse over my aching muscles as I washed the sweat and stink off my body and out of my hair. I luxuriated as long as I could under the warm spray before I decided I was just going to start pruning like some old biddy and got out.

Zane had left my bag on the rumpled bed. Along with a nice tray of toast with marmalade, tea and orange juice and, god love him, aspirin.

And a note.

Constable Richard Handcock is on his way to pick you up. – Robbie ♥♥♥.

PS- He sounded sexy as fuck! If he's as good looking as he sounds, I'd do him in a heartbeat!

I choked on the orange juice.

What the Fuck?

Chapter Five.

From my vantage point at the top of the stairs, I heard the front door open and Robbie welcome someone inside. *Cuntstable* Dick had arrived.

I wasn't nearly ready yet, still clad in my sports bra and a pair of boy-short style knickers, but I was curious to see why he had decided to come all this way out here from the village to pick me up and take me back to my car. Maybe he wanted to get a glimpse of Adam, who was filming in Scotland, so he had no chance there.

Mel was due back from a Doctor's appointment with her mum at any minute. Her due date was getting closer and she was getting worried, first time mum jitters. It didn't help that Mrs Del Rosa, Adam's birth mother, and her own mother had been fluttering around her. This was Mrs Whittaker's first grandchild.

I leaned over the railing a little, catching a glimpse of *Cuntstable* Dick in regular clothes. He wore a tight black tee-shirt that seemed almost painted on his body, and a pair of jeans that hugged his arse.

"Oh, My God! Sandbags required...like yesterday." Zane whispered beside me. I squealed in fright and pushed him back away from the railing. I grabbed his wrist and dragged him in my hobbling gait back to the guest room where I shut the door a little louder than I intended to.

"You little shite!" I slapped him playfully on his chest. "You scared the absolute fuck out of me. Fuck you and those fucking ninja skills." I stopped, then placed my hands back on his chest. "Holy fuck Zane, have you been working out?"

He grinned. "Maybe…"

"Oh God, don't tell me you've been thinking about that body building idea again?"

"Nope." He smirked. "I'm going to be the next top model." I rolled my eyes. "Don't you scoff at me young lady! I *was* going to ask if you could help me build my portfolio, but now, I'm not so sure." He took on an offended air about himself, sticking his nose up in the air.

"Oh, come the fuck on, Zane. I'll be happy to help you with your portfolio. Besides, it would help my own, especially if I want to get into runway and model photography. We can help each other."

Zane squealed and clapped his hands together in such a rapid motion it was a blur of sight and sound. "Yay!" he cheered. "I'm going to be a model!" He clasped my hands in his. "Oh, you won't regret this, at all! I have contacts back in LA, and we can get you started over there whenever you're ready." He looked me over. "But, sweetie, you need to get dressed, I don't think your constable is ready to see you nearly naked." He smirked. "Or maybe he is…"

I scowled. "*Cuntstable* Dick won't be seeing me nearly naked or otherwise anytime soon, if ever." I raised a finger to punch my point home.

Zane wrapped an arm around me and kissed me on the temple. "Darling, he can try, but I know you've got the resolve." He got up and moved to the bedroom door. "Now, you wait here, and I'll get you something nice of Mel's for you to wear."

"What's wrong with my clothes?" I asked, picking up my singlet top.

"Darling, have you seen those rags? They don't fit anymore. You've lost more weight this year. You need to eat a little more."

"Ugh." I moaned, flopping back onto the bed. Zane was back within a few minutes, holding up a skin tight pair of jeans and a low-cut top that put my not-so-ample cleavage on display.

"You're kidding me, right?" I asked him. Zane grinned and shook his head. "I fucking hate you, Fag." I grumbled, laying back on the bed and pulling the jeans up my legs. They stopped at the curve of my arse and refused to go any further. "They don't fucking fit!" I tugged again, my hand slipping off the hem.

"Here, let me help!" Zane said, helping me to stand. I kept my weight on my good foot, favouring the injured one while Zane gripped the hemline of the wretched jeans and tugged, jostling me up and down against his body. I faced him, chest to chest, my poor little c-cups smacking him in the face with each jostling attempt to get in my pants.

The door opened, and a throat cleared. Both Zane and my faces turned to see Robbie and *Cuntstable* Dick staring at us with looks of amusement and confusion.

"Gee, Zane, here I was thinking you were gay," Robbie said with a smirk. "I didn't think you batted for the other team."

"Oh, bite me, darling," Zane said poking his tongue out.

31

"I already did." Robbie retorted.

"I remember."

"Uh guys? Excuse me, half-dressed woman getting shoved into jeans that don't fit here… A little privacy please?" I said, turning away from the eyes of the boys. I had noticed that *Cuntstable* Dick's eyes had been riveted on me the whole time, almost like he wanted to shove Zane aside and do the job himself.

And you know what the stupid thing was? I'd have been more than happy to let him. Despite the fact that he was an arrogant arsehole, who gave me two tickets in one day, stole my keys, and then came to my best friends place to pick me up and take me back to my car.

I watched his arse as he turned away, my eyes glued to the jeans-clad glutes of the sexy pillock. My naughty mind went through the fantasies of what I could do to that body. My own started to respond to those dirty, naughty thoughts.

But seriously, brain? Have you lost all sensibilities? This guy was an A-Grade arse, and here I was fantasising about licking his pecs and abs while I dug my fingernails into his delectable arse.

Robbie closed the door with a smirk.

"Don't worry, darling, I was thinking about his sexy arse too." Zane grinned.

What. The. Fuck?!

Chapter Six.

I had changed from the jeans of death into a more comfortable pair of sweatpants, the kind I used when I was having a girls' night in with Mel and we'd be slumped over each other on the couch watching some silly comedy, like Monty Python or some sappy girly shit. But right now, I was sitting in the passenger seat of *Cuntstable* Dick's car as we drove through the beautiful countryside back towards the village.

"So…" he began, the awkwardness levels in the car were rising at an exponential rate.

"So…" I said back to him. The silence between us grew. He seemed to grip the steering wheel tighter.

"Okay. So, I may have come across as a bit of a pillock yesterday, but in all fairness, I am a police officer, and I was on duty. I was just doing my job," he said as he stopped at an intersection and turned on to the road that led to the village.

"Right," I said, not intending on saying anything more.

"In London, we do things a lot differently than here."

"Well, here's the thing, you're not in London anymore, Toto," I said, gazing out the window. "We are a bit more relaxed here, not everyone is out trying to break the law intentionally. You need to get that big spiky stick out of your arse and stop being such an arse. You'll last a bit longer than the last London copper that came through here."

"Why, what happened to the last transfer?"

"He went bonkers and ended up in Middlefield Mental Hospital."

"He what?" Dick looked at me, surprise on his face.

"Yup. Farmer Dawkins had an old, World War Two German bomb, from The Blitz, in one of his fields. Everyone knew about it, and it had been disarmed years ago, but he wanted it left there as a souvenir. This copper had given him five tickets in one week for parking his tractor in town while he went and did the shopping, he had no car you see, and the poor old farmer knew he couldn't afford to pay, so he called up the station and asked specifically for that officer to come over to his farm to help with something urgent." I paused in my story as we entered the town, looking around.

"And?" Dick prompted me.

"And the town heard about it, and all came out, even the off-duty coppers. He wasn't too popular with them either. Everyone watched while this poor sod started to look over the bomb, Dawkins even gave him a pair of wire clippers and told him he had to disarm it. The silly bugger reached forward with a hand and as soon as he touched the bomb, the onlookers all shouted *'BOOM!'*"

I giggled at the memory. I was one of those onlookers. Nearly everyone there had had a run-in with that particular tosser, and none-too-pleasant ones at that.

"He jumped so high, pissed his pants and ran screaming into the woods." I reached down and adjusted the bandage that was wrapped around my ankle. "It took us a day or two to find him. He was covered in dirt and manure and trembling like a leaf. Poor bastard kept mumbling about bombs and evil towns and the Germans. The doctor had him committed." I grinned wickedly. "So, the moral of the story, is don't piss off the townsfolk." I noticed we were pulling up beside my car. Dick smiled and handed me my keys.

"I'll remember that." He grinned, before he unbuckled his seatbelt and got out of the car. He came around to the passenger side as I opened the door and held out a hand. I eyed it a moment before taking it, letting him help me up. I hobbled a little, getting my balance.

"Are you going to be okay driving with your sore ankle?" he asked, helping me over to the driver's side of my car. His body was warm against me, and his scent was masculine and delicious. *Down girl!*

"I should be. I only live a few streets over," I said as I unlocked my car. Dick held open the door for me.

"I'll follow you home," he said.

I gave him a curious look, not sure what to make of his decision.

"To make sure you get home okay. I promise, I'm not one of those crazy stalkerish type cops," he said as I settled in my seat and put my seatbelt on.

"Oh-kay then…" I said slowly, still unsure as to what to make of him. He smiled at me as he closed the door and stepped back, letting me start my baby and pull away from the parking space where I'd abandoned her for the night. The pounding of the music set the local dogs off again. I checked my rear-view mirror to see him pull out in his sedan behind me.

A few turns later, we had pulled up in front of my row of flats. I was on the second floor, and not relishing the idea of climbing the steps to my flat. I got out, with *Cuntstable* Dick holding the door, and a hand out for me.

"Well, fuck me, chivalry ain't dead after all." I smirked.

"Was just raised to be a gentleman, I guess." He grinned.

"Oh, so it was the police force that turned you into a bit of a dick then?" I couldn't help myself.

"Nope, people in general did that," he said, closing my car door for me. "Which one is yours?" He looked up at the row of small flats.

"Number six," I said, nodding up to the one on the end of the second floor.

I began to hobble towards it. Dick was there in a second, his arm slipping under mine and around my back, as he tried to support me up the stairs.

"I'm injured, not fucking invalid." I snapped, feeling slightly insulted that he felt the need to burden himself with me. Still, he didn't let me go. And in some twisted fucking way, I was grateful. I was still unsteady as fuck on my injured ankle.

"I could carry you caveman style." He smirked, waggling his eyebrows.

"Fuck off." I groused. We made our way to my door where he finally released me, as I unlocked the door to my crappy flat. My cat, Lord Psycho, heard the keys and instantly began yowling for food.

"Okay, so here we are. Thanks for everything, except the tickets, and taking my keys," I said so quickly my words almost blended together in an unintelligible mash.

"I am sorry about the keys, but the tickets… I was—"

"Only doing your job, Yeah, yeah, I know." Lord Psycho, or LP, as I called him, yowled again, making a horrendous noise.

"Look, I feel we got off on the wrong foot here. You only get to make one first impression, and I feel like I've bollocksed it up." He sighed, running a hand over his shaven head. "I'd like to make it up to you. Would you like to come out for a coffee with me?"

It was cute, how he was trying to endear me to him, almost puppy-dog like with the eyes he was making at me. Pity, I was a cat person…and with LP, I was on my way to crazy cat lady status.

But seriously? After all that? He wanted to take me out for coffee?

What. The. Fuck?

Chapter Seven.

I was flummoxed. "Uh…okay, sure, I'll call you when I have the time," I said, quickly opening my door and letting myself in before he could see what a state my flat was in.

I shut the door behind me, pressed my back against the cheap plywood panelling and hid like a coward until I heard his heavy footsteps recede down the concrete walkway that joined the flats on the upper floor. I stayed like that until I heard him pull out of the driveway, peeking around the window like someone who had something to hide.

I so totally didn't. I watched him turn the corner, unable to tear my gaze from him driving away from me, out of my life. A small part of me hoped he'd call, but then I realised I didn't have his number, nor he mine. My mind began to drift with thoughts of how I could give him my digits. However, considering my track record with guys, was I really wanting to start a relationship with someone who was a bit of a pillock? The town copper?

It wouldn't work. There was no happy ending for me, the cards of fate just weren't ever right, I hated my family with a passion that I should have reserved for the stuck-up bitches at school. The ones who would bag me out for my high-school goth style, or my baggy clothes that hid the bruises after Dad threw me across the room in a drunken rage blaming me for Mum's infidelities and drug abuse.

My one escape had been Mel and her family. I was practically adopted by the Whittakers. There'd been more times than I could count that my parents had been at it. The music of fist against flesh, and the screams of drunken anger that caused me to flee out my window, risking the thorns from the scrabbly climbing rose that choked the rusting drainpipe I used to shimmy down to get out of the house in the darkness and across the fields, pushing my way through hedges and risking being shot at by farmers who thought I was a wild dog. I'm sure I looked wild enough with bloodied arms and legs, twigs wild in my unkempt hair. My pain was worth a little bit of love and normalcy from a family not my own.

My own family were arseholes. I seemed to attract the same.

A sharp claw jolted me away from my forlorn thoughts.

I was already in a relationship with an arsehole. A fucking cat who 'owned' me.

"What? Oh, fuck LP. Okay, okay, I got you," I said picking up the four-legged feline I had been cursed with and getting him something to eat.

I'd found him as an abandoned kitten on one of my last nights living under my parents' roof. The scrawny, near feral kitten had snuck into my dad's run-down shed. I'd had enough and wanted to finish my life using weed killer or, faster, and probably less painful, the axe cutting across my wrists, having hit my lowest point.

I'd acted out as a teen, gotten into some alcohol one night at a party and wound up sleeping with two guys…one who hadn't worn a condom. By the second month of not getting my period, I knew…well, that and the 'stomach flu' I seemed to have. I went into town, after swiping some drugs from my mum's secret stash, she didn't think I knew about, sold them to some kids I knew were into the ecstasy pills Mum had hidden from 'Daddy dearest', and went to the local pharmacy, where I purchased my first pregnancy test.

My bitch of a mother had found the pregnancy test, and told Dad, who then proceeded to 'beat the little bastard out of me', as the fucking prick so eloquently put it. Dad threw me in the shed and put a lock on it. In the tiny pinpricks of light that shone through the nail holes in the shed, I discovered I was bleeding. I cried, I was ashamed, but I wanted that poor baby to have a better life than I did, and I had been determined to make sure it had that.

Because of my cunt of a father, I was not going to be a mum. But I could give this scrawny little kitten what my unborn baby could never have. Love, and a safe home to live in.

I managed to break out of the shed using one of the older metal walls, which had begun to curl away from the old wood, snuck into the house where the arseholes, who were my parents were sleeping off their drunken states, packed my shit and began living in an abandoned warehouse taking Lord Psycho with me. Mel had given me a camera for Christmas, one of those cheap polaroid type ones, and she'd given me extra film for it too. She'd even offered to let me live in her room with her. I declined. I needed to find myself, discover who I was, for me. I still loved her, still needed her as my best friend.

It was my eighteenth birthday when Danny came into my life. He had been my saving grace. I was taking photographs of areas around the village, scenic spots, while avoiding the poor side of town where I knew my asshole parents still lived. I took pictures until my camera film ran out, taking each polaroid and shaking it in the air to let it develop before I checked it over and slipped it into a stolen plastic sleeve for protection.

I sold my better ones for a few pounds, so I could get something to eat, most of my meagre dinners were dumpster dives, and LP managed to get a few rodents in our abandoned warehouse to keep him a happy kitty, though he did mooch off me a little bit.

Danny found me in my little warehouse, tracking me down, after he bought two of my polaroids. I was sceptical of him at first, this stranger offering me a job, in which I didn't have to lick, suck or fuck anything, just take pictures, and he'd teach me how to become a professional photographer.

He saw potential in the scrawny girl who stank to high heaven, and clutched a wriggling cat in her arms like he was a safety blanket, no matter if he scratched up her face.

I owed Danny so much.

I had my career to think of. I went to the door of the small bathroom that also acted as my dark room. It was perfect, no windows to allow that pesky sun in, and decent ventilation from the ceiling exhaust fan when I was working with chemicals. I had a few pictures hanging up, left drying from my last shoot, ones I was happy with and going to sell at the market on the weekend.

Though there was something not quite right, the bathroom door was ajar, I know I'd closed it when I left yesterday. I slowly pushed open the door and switched on the light.

I gasped in horror.

The pictures had all been shredded. Great jagged strips torn from the photographic paper. There was only one culprit who could be so dastardly as to do this.

And the tabby little fucker was contentedly licking his paws after a good meal of sardines.

"LP!" I shouted, turning to face the guilty party. I'm sure my face was a picture of insane rage at the furry little fucker.

"WHAT THE FUCK!?"

Chapter Eight.

The fucking cunt of a cat! I ran at him, anger fuelling my mind and clouding my judgment. Of course, being uninjured and having full use of four legs, *and* being a cat, the little sod managed to evade my hobbling gait and snarling promises of turning him into a fur rug to sit in front of the little fan heater that barely heated the place, but shot my power bills up to the fucking moon in winter.

I chased him around until I gave up. He was too quick, nimble and smart for me. I fell face-first on the sofa, my legs kicked up behind me as I groaned. I was hoping to have these pictures framed and ready for sale today. It seemed like my luck was running out.

Unlucky in love – check.

Unlucky with work – kinda check.

Unlucky in general – check, check-fuckity-check.

I lay there, my face buried in the pillow that was covered in a fine layer of cat fur. Thank fuck I wasn't allergic or the little fucker would have never stood a chance. I felt the sofa cushion in front of me dip suddenly, a soft purring and the tip of a small, wet nose pushing against my exposed forehead, before the rest of LP's face pushed against me in that affectionate way cats had of rubbing themselves all over you.

"You're lucky I love you, you fucker," I said, looking up. I instantly regretted it. I was greeted with LP's favourite pose. 'The-cat's-arse-in-the-human's-face'. Oh, how many times had I woken up to that sweet little view in the morning… That or a claw-n-paw to the face.

"*Really* lucky I love you," I grumbled to the pussy's pucker.

A few hours later I sat at my tiny kitchen table, the shreds of photographic paper laid out on a stiff, piece of white cardboard canvas. With a stick of glue in hand, I worked painstakingly on the pieces, but I didn't glue them back together, instead I let my inner artist have at it.

I finished the picture and within, it seemed like I saw a part of my soul. I hadn't realised, that in the background, I'd inadvertently captured the old two-storey cottage where my parents had lived, where my hellish childhood had drawn out, long and desolate. The house had been torn in two by LP's savage claws. It seemed poetic, that I was trying to put back together that which had been shattered in the first place, my childhood home.

I'd left space between the jagged pieces of the picture, like pieces of a puzzle that would never fit again, bits missing, the heart and soul of the place gone forever, or perhaps it was never there to start with. I gazed at the black and white image, shiny photographic paper against dull canvas. It was raw, gritty, and showed the reality, with the fantasy of my life, washed white behind the lies my parents told the police, the school and the social workers.

I felt the first hot, angry tear fall. I hadn't fucking cried in a long time. Not over those fuckers, not over that fucking house where I was supposed to feel safe, but where I had nothing but fear and loathing burning through my veins each time I had to push the rusty gate open after school.

My parents no longer lived there. Dad had drunk himself into liver failure and then died in prison after assaulting a police officer, and Mum had left him to be with one of her 'boyfriends' shortly after he went to prison. I'd learned she'd overdosed a few weeks after he died. I didn't attend their funerals, nor did I attend the reading of their wills. I didn't want anything from them ever again.

I still had the unopened letter from Mum's lawyer. Mr Montgomery had even come to my flat, telling me I now owned the cottage, as the last living descendant of my mother's line.

I didn't want it. Never did. Now it stood empty, and abandoned. Like my heart.

I should sell it, be done with that part of my life. But something within me, just couldn't bear to part with it. It was still part of me. My pain, my suffering. The loss of my baby. Mel knew about so much of my agony, but not about my miscarriage. Only I knew about that. I'd never told anyone about it. I still felt the shame, the failure of not being able to protect my unborn child from the wrath of a drunken cunt of a father, and the vindictiveness of a bitch of a mother.

Every time I looked at that house, I felt every strike of that cunt's fists. Every visit from the police or the social workers, every lie they told to keep me there, so they could get the most out of a system that supported the abusive fuckers that they were. To hell with the poor girl inside who hid the bruises beneath the baggy clothes that her sodding excuses for parents said were the fashion she liked.

I looked at the picture. The more I looked at it, the angrier I got, and the happier I was that LP had destroyed that one picture, that in another person's eyes, would have been so beautiful, so homely. All I saw, all I felt, was hate.

47

I picked up the piece of cardboard canvas, stomping out of my little boxy flat and down the steps, ignoring the ache on my injured ankle and down to the dumpster out the back. I shoved the attempt at...whatever the fuck I was trying to accomplish deep down into the dumpster.

I had no idea what was going through my mind when I tried to fix the past. But ya know? I tried, but seriously,

What the Fuck?

Chapter Nine.

"Okay, so we have Mr and Mrs Flannigan's Gold Wedding Anniversary coming up. They want us to re-create their wedding pictures. Though I think there's about three members of the wedding party who aren't alive any longer, but we do have pictures of them available to us, so we can photoshop them in with the permission of the family members." Danny looked up from the appointments book. I nodded, taking notes down. I had learned a bit of photoshop, enough that I knew I didn't like the 'modern' day thing of 'photoshopping' shit in.

"Friday, we have the local debutante ball. Saturday, we have three weddings, so we'll have to split for the first two in the morning. Then we have the big one in the afternoon. Sunday," he paused, looking at me…

"Sunday, I have the market booked," I said, shifting my feet off the desk and stomping the carpeted floor under my chair.

We were sitting in Danny's office, actually a converted conservatory in his little row house cloistered amongst the others in a cul-de-sac off the main road. The week had progressed slowly, I'd taken my SLR and Polaroid cameras out and about, shooting bits and pieces of the countryside, houses that were favourites, bridges, cows, the usual nature-y shit that sold at the markets to the touristy types.

I'd been visiting Mel a few times through the week, taking the last of her progressing pregnancy photographs. Adam had come back from Scotland, and was back at the Castle, filming the third movie in the 'Duke' series. The set of the first one was where he had first met Mel, who had

49

become the unlucky recipient of a broken heel and a bowl of chilled punch, a result of said heel. The subsequent, and leaked video of her spectacular fall from grace had brought them closer together, and from that disaster, and a few others, they lost and then found each other here in England after Mel's dad had a stroke.

The photographs that they selected, were then given to me to 'officially' sell to the media. Thus, I was technically their official photographer. I took some happy snaps, candid shots, the usual stuff. Shots of them before they got into their limo to go to gala events, charity fundraisers all that fucking superstar jazz that Mel now had to deal with.

I loved seeing her happy though. It was something I didn't think I deserved, despite her telling me I did. With all the shite I'd gone through, I highly doubted it. Hell, I hadn't even seen *Cuntstable* Dick over the last week, and I knew he was out and about, because there were a few people griping about the 'new copper' on the local beat. I smirked at that, then felt my body flush at the memory of him in that tight shirt… Fuck, I needed to get laid. My vibe was out of batteries, and I was overdue to any kind of satisfaction, even if it was just battery-operated satisfaction.

"Libby? Are you listening to me? Earth to Libby?"

"Huh?" I asked, jolting out of my daydream.

"The local Fireman, Paramedic and Policeman's ball committee wants a photographer to work at their annual ball in two weeks' time. I've got a visit planned with Lonnie then, so I'll have to get you to do it for me.

"Oh… Uh… Okay, no problem." I knew Danny tried to spend as much time with his sweet little three-year-old as he could. He and his girlfriend, Shelly, had separated not long after Shelly had discovered she was pregnant with Danny's baby. Despite them trying to reconcile for the sake of little Lonnie, it just never worked out, so they separated again. When Shelly moved back to her parent's place, over three hours away, it almost broke Danny, but he was determined to live his life and keep Lonnie in it, so they figured out a compromise. They both drove an hour and a half to Danny's Mum's home, where Danny and Lonnie would stay for a weekend before Shelly would come and pick up Lonnie.

"Chin up, old duck. You might find yourself a nice sexy policeman or a hot fireman, maybe even a paramedic to restart that heart of yours."

I scowled at him and flipped him the bird. He knew all about my encounter with *Cuntstable* Dick. The fucker had even laughed harder when I told him about my keys being nicked by the dick.

"Right," he continued. "So, you have the keys to the gallery. The exhibits are all ready to go, but the big question is, are you ready for tonight?"

I sighed. Tonight was not going to change my life, but having pieces in an exhibit that we'd put together with the local artist community was a big deal, at least for me.

I'd never had any of my photographs up for others to see, well, other than the customers of course. But Danny, being the awesome fucker that he was, went through my old portfolio of landscapes and candids and demanded that I put them in the exhibition.

"I guess," I mumbled, picking at the fraying armrest of the chair I sat in. I sighed. "Yeah, okay I'm ready." I didn't sound too convincing, even to myself.

Danny leaned forward, his deep blue eyes piercing beneath the mop of dirty blonde hair.

"Listen, Kid," he said, using the nickname he branded me with when he found me shivering with cold in the warehouse with LP clutched against me for a semblance of warmth, despite the threadbare blankets I had wrapped around us to keep us warm. "You got this. You have a talent I've not seen in a long time. You have an eye for detail and beauty that is unmatched by any other photographer I know." He put a reassuring hand on my shoulder. "You got this, Libby, I know you do. You need to put all your doubts out of your mind." He grinned. "And if no-one buys your work, then you know what? Fuck 'em."

"Yeah, fuck 'em," I muttered, still not one-hundred percent sold on his enthusiasm. I downed my cup of tea that had been sitting, cooling on the desk and stood up. "Right, I guess I'd better go get tarted up then."

"I'll see you later. And you'll do great."

***

I smiled at the people who milled around, looking over sculptures and artworks in the form of paintings, prints, textile weavings and my photographs. There was a large group of people milling around one of my pieces in particular, though I knew all of the pieces that were in here, there was one that I knew I hadn't submitted… The one that everyone was 'ooh-ing' and 'aah-ing' over. I walked

52

up to the group, slowly pushing my way through so I could get a better look at it.

My heart fell through the pit of my stomach and I felt sick.

It was the carboard canvas piece that I'd unceremoniously dumped in the rubbish. And it had a 'sold' card sticking against the frame.

For three hundred fucking pounds!

What. The. Fuck?!

Chapter Ten.

I spun, pushing my way out of the crowd. I couldn't breathe. I needed air, needed to get the fuck out of the little former corner shop-turned-gallery. My heart pounding hard in my chest as I bolted out the door, hearing Mel and Adam calling out to me, Danny's voice floated by as I bolted. My feet pounded the pavement beneath me as I escaped into the night.

Hot, angry tears traced down my cheeks at the thought of people seeing the place where I was hurt so many times in my youth and childhood. Seen as a piece of art, that someone liked so much they'd pay that amount of money, hell any amount of money to buy it. It felt like every harsh word, every strike of my father's fists against my body were there again, tenfold.

I felt the pain in my stomach, my heart, my soul all over again as I lost the baby. I ran blindly through the streets until I came to the one place I never wanted to set foot in, or see again.

The cottage.

It stood forlorn in the dim moonlight. My breath was ragged as I pushed open the rusty gate. Its hinges, unoiled and weathered through the years screeched harshly, as if the monsters within the house could be awoken again. I knew they were no longer alive in the old clay brick and mortar cottage, nothing but ashes in the wind, and bones beneath the ground; but the fuckers were well and truly alive in my mind. Their claws had secured their place in my soul and even though I knew they couldn't hurt me anymore, I still felt each and every cruelty they unleashed on me.

I looked over the hated dwelling. My fingers curling and twitching. I stumbled over a chunk of concrete, hand sized and perfect. I knew no-one lived there, after all, I owned the place and refused to rent it out. The waist-high grass was a testament to the fact that this house had become as abused, neglected and unloved as I had been. I gripped the chunk and hurled it at the house. It hit one of the windows that hadn't been broken or boarded up already. The shattering of the glass sounding loud in the cool darkness of the spring night. It was the sound of my first chain breaking. I laughed, a dry, throaty chuckle that bordered on near-fucking hysterical insanity.

I walked to the shed, it was already half-collapsed with the weathering it had endured. I knew there was an old axe in there. I had considered using the sharp blade to cut my wrists and end it all as I lost my baby. I pushed through the place where the corrugated iron had separated, ignoring the nails that tore my dress and scratched my skin. My goal was in sight.

The holes where the roof of the shed had collapsed had exposed the axe to the weather. The head was rusted and no longer sharp. I didn't need it for the cutting edge. I needed it to destroy the house that held me prisoner for so long.

I started with the shed. My body swinging the axe like a sledgehammer, my muscles bunching and releasing with each heavy, soul-freeing strike. I cried out as the axe head struck the rotten wood of the shed and destroyed it with vigour.

My face was wet from the tears I'd shed, the sky above was clear, the stars and the moon were my only witnesses. Sweat ran in rivulets down my body, over my neck and between the cleavage of my breasts as I heaved and swung the axe again, and again, and again, destroying the place where my heart and soul had finally shattered. Destroying the chains that kept me in the one memory that haunted me. The fucking shed.

"Libby…" A voice called to me through my emotional pain. I fumbled with the axe, splinters burrowing their way into the flesh of my palms. I sobbed, my legs trembled with adrenalin and exhaustion, both emotional and physical as I sank to the dew-damp grass.

Warm hands caressed my shoulders as I broke.

"It's okay, Libby, I got you." I heard the voice of *Cuntstable* Dick, warm and soothing.

His hands left me for a moment, and I sobbed, bereft of the contact, before he gently took the axe from my hands and covered my bare shoulders with his jacket. I was lifted into his strong arms and carried to a car. I settled, quietly sobbing in the passenger seat, as he drove us away from the cottage where I tried to break free of my demons. Through the haze of my misery, I heard him speaking on the phone. I ignored the world until he slowed.

He pulled up outside a small block of flats. I knew them to be the temporary residences that belonged to the police station, for new officers who didn't have families and the need for a permanent home just yet. It meant that maybe *Cuntstable* Dick wasn't staying as long as was first thought. He helped me out of the car, and before I could protest, he swept his arm under my leg and carried me bridal style to his flat, unlocking the door and carrying me inside.

He jostled me slightly in his arms as he flipped the light on. Warm, yellow light illuminated the darkness as my blurry eyes adjusted. The place was spartan, there were still boxes stacked against one wall of the small flat, obviously unpacking wasn't a priority for him.

He settled my feet on the floor and guided me to the kitchen table, noticing my hands were curled up in pain from the splinters I'd taken.

"Have a seat, I'll just grab the first aid kit," he said, leaving me to move to the bathroom.

"That's really not necessary," I said, my voice tight from my hysterics.

I must have looked a fright. I knew my mascara had run, my eyes felt red and puffy, and my nose was running like a faucet. I absently wiped the back of my hand against my nose, leaving a smear of snot on my skin. Dick came back with a box of tissues, a warm damp wash cloth, and the white box with the green first aid symbol on it.

He carefully took my chin in warm, with his slightly calloused fingers, and wiped the mess from my cheeks and upper lip with the wash cloth.

"You had quite a few people worried about you, Libby," he said softly, taking the cloth and wiping my smear of snot from the back of my hand.

Carefully he turned my hand over and looked at the redness, and the little black splinters that had embedded themselves in my hands. He took out a pair of tweezers and some antiseptic wipes, placing them beside my hand on the table.

"Okay, this will hurt, but you're a tough girl. I mean you sure showed that shed what for." He smirked, taking up the tweezers. I winced. "Oh, come on, I haven't even started yet." He grinned, before he pressed the nose of the tweezers against my skin, pushing the first splinter out.

I whimpered, and sucked in a breath at the sharp pain "Didn't know you were such a sadist," I griped.

"One of my more endearing qualities, I assure you." He smirked, taking the splinter and wiping it off the tweezers onto a tissue, before going for the next one.

"Your friend, Danny said he'd come collect you shortly. I just want to make sure you're okay before I hand you over." He looked at the big splinter in the tweezer's grip. "That's a big bugger."

I nodded, biting my lip against the sting.

His eyes locked on mine. "So, why were you destroying that shed?"

I paled, my throat closed up and I began to tremble a little.

"Libby?" His eyes showed his concern. "It's okay, you're safe." Dick had gone back into policeman mode. "No-one is going to hurt you, okay?" he asked, his hands gripping mine. I yelped, there were still a couple of splinters in there.

"Oh, fuck! Sorry." He lifted my hands to his lips and kissed them... He fucking *kissed* them. I sat there, my mouth agape, surprise must have been scrawled all over my face in permanent marker. Dick stopped, pulled my hands from his lips. "Oh, uh...right." He blushed. "Sorry." His cheeks flushed sweetly. He was silent as he went about, plucking the rest of the splinters from my flesh until Danny arrived…With a certain picture tucked under his arm.

"Hey Richard, here's your purchase, thanks for finding our girl."

My eyes went wide as I saw that fucking photograph. I almost stopped breathing as Danny handed it over to *Cuntstable* Dick.

"Thanks." He smiled. "It's really a beautiful piece, perfect in its imperfect form."

I gaped, looking at the fucker who had bought a piece of my shattered past and said it was perfect.

What. The. FUCK?!

Chapter Eleven.

"I can't fucking believe you did that, you're a fucking arsehole." I snapped at Danny as he drove us back to my flat. I'd left *Cuntstable* Dick's place without saying goodbye, or thanking him for taking the splinters out of my aching hands. "I threw that fucking piece of shite picture out for a reason, Danny!" The pillock just let me rant at him, his hands resting easily on the steering wheel as he drove. "And then you *sold* it to that fucking *Cuntstable*. Seriously, Danny! You know what that place means to me, you know about the shit that went on in that house. Why would you fucking do that? I never wanted to see that picture again."

"That may be, Libby. But it was, as he said, beautiful, perfect in its imperfection. You are a broken soul, still putting yourself back together. Sure, there might be a chip off here or there off your hard-won veneer, but Libby, you are an artist. And how many artists have had a broken soul? Their imperfections are their saving grace, their healing comes out in their creativity." He turned a corner, entering my street. "You have a gift, borne of tragedy and heartbreak. Don't throw it away." He reached into his pocket and handed me over a thousand pounds in notes and cheques. "That's from your sales tonight." He smiled. "Get yourself something nice." He stopped at my drive. I got out of the car and turned to face him.

"You're still a pillock," I said softly. My head had started to pound with a slight ache from the emotional stress.

"I know." He grinned. "Now go get some rest."

I nodded, turning away as he drove off. I noticed the front light was still on at my front door, which was expected, but I didn't expect the lights to be on, glowing behind my closed curtains. I slipped up the stairs to my front door, slowly sliding the key in and unlocking the door, knowing the click would alert any would-be robber to my return. I pushed the door open quickly, a girlish squeal erupted from one of the two figures making out on my couch.

"Jesus fucking Christ Mel! You scared me half to death," I said stepping inside my flat. Mel quickly pulled the skirt of her gown down over her knees,

"Sorry, Libby, we were waiting for you to come home, Adam—"

"Adam didn't want his heavily pregnant wife roaming around the countryside hunting for her best friend in the dark, so I convinced her to come here and wait," Adam said, not even bothering to fix his unbuttoned shirt.

"Then…the pregnancy hormones kicked in…"

"And you've been hornier than a bitch in heat, I get it," I said, flopping down in the mismatched armchair. "But seriously? On my fucking couch? You know how much I could sell that for now, right? 'The couch that Adam Jacobs made out with his pregnant wife on'," I said with a dramatic wave of my hand, as if I was imagining the words on a billboard to advertise said couch. "It'd sell for millions." I smirked.

Adam chuckled. "Yeah, maybe billions. You'd be rich beyond your wildest dreams.

I laughed. "Yeah, right. Only if you left a little white stain or two on there."

"Eww! Libby! Don't talk about my husband's white stains, he'll get a big head on him."

Adam leaned forward and whispered something against her ear. Mel blushed and slapped him playfully on the chest.

"Nope, so don't want to know what he said." I pushed myself up from the sunken cushion of my armchair and headed to the kitchen. "Tea?"

"Decaf for milady, and I'll have a coffee if you got it."

I snorted. "Coffee." I pulled three mugs from the cupboard. "What do you think this is? A fucking Starbucks?"

Fortunately, I did have coffee, and I did have decaffeinated tea bags just for Mel. Mel had come and visited me often while Adam was away on set. We'd sit on my shitty couch and watch crappy movies, LP snuggled up between us, purring contentedly.

I made my guests their hot drinks, and brought the cups out with a plate of biscuits.

"Okay, so tell me, what the hell happened tonight, Libby?" Mel asked, clutching her tea in her hands while Adam sat back with an arm draped over Mel's shoulders.

"The fucking cottage," I said, sighing as I sat back against the lumpy backrest.

"The cottage?" Adam asked, curious.

"Yep, the fucking cottage. The place where I grew up, or was dragged up, depending on how you see it."

I didn't know what Mel had told him, from the look on her face, it wasn't much, and I was secretly pleased about that. It meant that my best friend, my confidante, still held my absolute trust. I sighed, then began to tell them about the picture I'd taken, how LP had destroyed it, and a few other pictures that weren't salvageable, and how I'd tried to piece back together the shattered past in an image that seemed to haunt me, just as much as that *fucking Cuntstable* Dick did.

Mel listened and didn't judge. She'd been there so many times in our youth, helping me up through her bedroom window, pulled out a box of band-aids, iodine and cotton balls, she'd kept under her bed for my visits, and tended to me like a nurse. Then we'd both curl up in her bed and talk about things that mattered, things that didn't remind me of my hell back at the fucking cottage.

She knew it all, except for the one thing that I kept to myself.

"But why the shed? I mean I can understand smashing the window, but why did you destroy the shed?" Mel asked.

My throat closed up, memories of laying curled up on the dusty concrete floor after the miserable fucking excuse I had for a father locked me in, after beating me and kicking my stomach until I was near insensate with the pain, then the sticky, wetness that bled out from between my legs. Mel could see there was something about the way my eyes shimmered with tears.

She turned to Adam. "Honey, can you give us a moment?" she asked, then pushed a little bit to get herself up off the sofa, Adam helping her, supporting her.

I was desperate for someone to show me the affection he showed her, but I knew I was too damaged for that.

Mel held her hand out to me. "Come on, I think you've been hiding something from me for a long time, and you need to let it out."

The sadness in Mel's eyes showed me she had an idea about what I wanted to tell her, I was so afraid. But as soon as the door was closed, and we settled on the bed. My loss, which still haunted me, so many years after the fact, pushed its way past my final barriers, breaking my heart all over again, shredding my soul. I sobbed against the swelling of life that waited in my best friend's belly as she held me.

"I knew your dad was a bastard, but seriously…" Mel said, as she stroked my hair, the next words spoken summed his actions up perfectly.

"What the fuck?"

Chapter Twelve.

Adam stood at my bedroom door. "Sorry, Libby, Sorry, Mel. I just wanted to make sure you were okay, I didn't mean to hear the last bit, but fuck," he said softly, lowering his head.

I knew he was worried about what kind of father he'd be, especially after finding out he was adopted not too long ago. It was one of the things that had Mel doubting his fidelity, especially when pictures of a beautiful woman and a child popped up in the papers with him. The woman and child turned out to be his half-sister and niece. I'd tried desperately to stop Mel from looking at the pictures, but it had been too late, and she'd had a category eleventy-bazillion meltdown.

"Honey, I'm going to stay here tonight," Mel said, huffing as she sat up a little on the bed, her arm around my shoulders, fingers stroking my arm.

"Okay, baby," Adam said. "I'll crash on the couch."

"No, you guys don't have to do that. That's not fair to you two," I said up, wiping my eyes. "I'll be fine."

"Shut up Libby," Mel said with a smirk. "It's what best friends do. Besides, you'll be called upon for babysitting duties soon," she said, rubbing her hand over her swollen belly. "Oh, he's kicking!"

She grabbed my hand and placed it over her belly. The flutter became a jolt as the baby kicked hard enough for us to not only feel it, but to see the lump of movement under her tight dress. Mel's eyes met mine.

"You'll be a fucking awesome mum," I said, knowing it would be true.

"So will you, one day," Mel promised me. Adam left us in the bedroom, I heard him pottering about in the kitchen, washing the mugs we'd used and putting them away after drying.

"You got him well trained then?" I asked.

Mel giggled. "Very well trained." She sighed. "Sorry about that pillock and his wife. Plenty more fish in the sea for our madam shark to devour." She grinned at her nickname for me.

I'd gone as a nurse shark to their last Halloween party…a slutty nurse shark. It was a tacky costume, a shark costume with a naughty nurse getup I'd bought as a lark at an adult store in London, but heck, it worked. I had a very good night, picked up a very sexy American footballer, who was dressed as a fisherman, and I'd let him hook and reel me in all night long. I couldn't help but laugh at the memory.

"See, got you to smile." She made a fist and gently nudged me with it. "Slapper."

"Tart."

"Skank"

"Ho."

We grinned. I hugged her. She was my best friend, and she knew all my terrible secrets, my shame, and she didn't judge. She had mourned with me now, knowing about my loss. Some might have said it wasn't to be, some might have even been so cruel as to say it was only two months along, it wasn't really there, but to me, as soon as I knew I was pregnant, I wanted it. I kept my hand on Mel's baby bump, feeling the restless little bugger shifting until he settled.

"This kid is going to be one very loved and cherished child."

"Especially by his Godmother." Mel grinned, giving me a knowing look. As far as I knew, they'd not asked anyone to be the godparents yet.

"Wait... What?"

"Adam, can you come in here a minute?" she called out. Adam was there in seconds.

"Everything okay, baby?" he asked, concern on his face.

"Yes, just want you here for this," Mel said, patting the side of the bed. She took his hand in hers when he sat beside her, before taking my free hand in her other hand. "We want you to be our baby's Godmother."

I couldn't believe it. I opened and closed my mouth a few times before I took a deep breath and gathered myself.

"I'm... Wow, speechless. Of course, I'd be fucking happy, and honoured to," I said.

My smile split my face, all previous sorrows forgotten for the moment as we enjoyed the happiness that my friends had given me. Mel hugged me tight, an awkward embrace with her belly in the way.

"Do you have some blankets and a spare pillow? I'll take the couch. You ladies share the bed," Adam said standing up.

"Guys, like I said, that's not necessary, go home. You'll both be more comfortable there." Mel looked at me, seeing I was determined that they shouldn't stay, especially as my bed was comfortable to me, but not quite to Mel in her delicate condition.

"Libby…" she said slowly.

"Mel…" I said shaking her head. "I'm a big girl, I'll be fucking fine."

"There you have it, she's almost back to normal." Mel grinned.

"Fuck normal." I grinned. "Look, you two get going, before the paps have a field day when they discover you're visiting a friend. God forbid you do something 'normal' like you know, us regular folks?"

I stood up, Adam helped Mel off the bed.

"Are you sure?" she asked, still looking at me with concerned eyes.

"I'll be fine. Besides, I have LP with me," I said, nodding to the cat, who was fast asleep in his basket.

Mel looked at Adam, then back at me. "Okay then," she said, as she gathered her bag, and Adam helped her with her jacket. "But if you need us, call, and we'll be right back, okay?"

"I will, I promise," I said letting them out of my home.

I watched from my door as Adam helped Mel down the steps, down to the black Range Rover that Mel never drove. I waved as they pulled out, Adam tooting the horn a couple of times in farewell. I headed back inside and settled down on the couch, dozing off to some terrible late-night telly.

I was woken with a fright when there was a banging on my door. I checked the time on my phone, it was after midnight.

I gripped my trusty cricket bat that I kept beside the front door, peeping through the eyehole before I unlocked and opened the door.

The multicoloured highlights of Zane's wild hair blazed under the front light.

"Zane!" I greeted him, with a speck of confusion "It's after midnight," I said, stepping aside to let him in. He carried in bags of junk food, and a couple of DVDs.

"I heard you needed some company. I couldn't sleep, so, I thought I'd come around. You look like you need some crappy, sappy Rom-Coms and lots and lots of chocolate."

I smirked, closing the door behind him. "Aw, what the fuck."

Chapter Thirteen.

After that first night, Zane had been around almost every night that week. He even came by to help me set up for this morning's market, before he saw a guy, who in his words was, 'OMG, that guy is so fucking HAWT!', and he went on the prowl. His mission: to see if he could get the guy's number, leaving me alone at my stall with all my framed and unframed photographs. I had cards and flyers set out as well, advertising Danny's photography business.

The spring morning sunshine beat down on the market. Tourists, who were here to see if they could catch a glimpse of the famous movie stars who were filming at the Castle, milled around the stalls of local produce and crafts. Our little village was having a bit of a boom time, even some of the local cafes were doing a great trade, and there were plans to renovate the local fish n' chip shop, upgrading the old fryers and the warped, laminated tables that were fixtures from at least the fifties.

I was helping a little old lady look over some of the photographs of the local area when I saw him. *Cuntstable* Dick. He was on duty, patrolling around the markets on foot with Lisa. He smiled when he saw me at my stall.

I glared.

He gave me puppy dog eyes.

I still glared.

He moved on. Lisa walked past, while he slipped around another stall. Then I saw the reason they had split, a young man had slipped his hand into a woman's bag and lifted her phone and purse from within, slipping the phone into his jacket pocket, and quickly slipping the notes from her purse before he dropped it and kicked it under a stall. I watched, while trying to make a sale with the old biddy, as Lisa and *Cuntstable* Dick moved to where the pickpocket was trying for another unsecured handbag. I returned my attention to my customer.

I looked up from the pictures that the old lady was looking at as shouting caught my ears. The pickpocket was running through the market, back towards my stall, arms and legs pumping as he pushed his body in a burst of adrenalin-fuelled speed.

"Excuse me, just a moment," I said to the lady, as I stepped out from behind my stall into the path of the pickpocket.

He was too busy looking behind him to see how far behind Lisa and Dick were to notice I had stepped in his way. I casually put out a foot as hc barrelled past, catching his foot and tripping him up. He stumbled and fell, face planting the cobblestone-styled bitumen of the blocked off street with an *'oomph!'*. I watched as Lisa and Dick slowed down, and stopped next to the pickpocket. *Cuntstable* Dick sat on the pickpocket's lower back, straddling him as he cuffed the criminal. Lisa pulled on a pair of gloves, ready to search him.

One of the other stall holders came over with the pilfered wallet that the pickpocket had kicked away to hide it.

Cuntstable Dick looked at me with a smirk as he hauled up the now hapless crook. "Good job, Libby. You'd make a pretty decent police officer," he said with a wink as Lisa started to search the guy.

I snorted and rolled my eyes, turning back to the old lady who was now more than happy to purchase a framed print.

"OMG, what did I miss?" Zane asked, coming up beside me with a bag of popcorn as I wrapped the framed print in an old newspaper to protect the frame for the old lady.

"Libby was doing some freelance police work," Dick said, with a smirk as Lisa finished checking over the pickpocket. All in all, they'd found a large sum of cash, credit cards and three phones on him.

"This looks like one of the guys we've been after for a while. Good job, Libby," Lisa said with a grin as she checked over the pickpocket's ID.

Cuntstable Dick nodded. "We'll need you to come down to the station to make a statement," he said to me.

"I can come later this afternoon, when we've packed up." I had no intention of doing this with him in a small interview room, plus I had a wedding shoot this afternoon.

"That's okay, I'll take care of your stall sweetheart, you just go with the nice officers," Zane said, pushing me towards Dick in a not-so-subtle way. I gave him my absolute best *'I'm gonna fucking kill you'* look.

"Great, we'll see you at the station in about half an hour." Dick smiled as he and Lisa hauled the pickpocket off towards their patrol car.

I turned slowly, with deadly precision. "Zane. You are a bitch."

75

"Why, thank-you sweetheart, now you better go get sorted, you look a little flustered. Go make yourself look absolutely sexy for that gorgeous policeman. I'm sure you'll break your nookie drought very soon." Zane grabbed my backpack and shooed me away from my stall.

I just stood there and looked at him, mouth agape, and with, what I was certain was a shocked look on my face. "Zane! Seriously?"

"Oh, come on, like I can't see the signs. You need to get laid, sister. And in such a bad way too. You've been twitchy, bitchy and totally hormonal. If I didn't know it wasn't your time of the month, I'd have guessed it was!" Zane chuckled.

"What…?" I gasped.

"Oh honey, I've known you for a while now, and I'm damned well attuned to you, and my girl Mel. If I was a chick, we'd totally be in sync with each other."

"Ugh, Zane, can you stop talking about that, like really?"

"What? It's a perfectly natural occurrence in a woman's biology. Besides, you seriously need to get some 'Dick' in you," he said with a wink.

"Zane! What the fuck?"

Chapter Fourteen.

I trudged up the brickwork steps to the police station, my backpack slung over my shoulder. I'd left the market reluctantly, after Zane assured me he'd take care of everything, including packing up the stall and having Robbie pick him and my stock up in the van to take back to Danny's studio, where we usually stored my market stock.

I pushed open the glass doors, the smell of paper and tea strong in my nose as I walked up to the desk.

"Hi Kev," I said with a smile for PC Kevin Harris. He was a red-haired bloke with freckles across his nose and a youthful look about him, though he was in his later thirties.

"'Ello Libby, hear you been trying to do some police work of your own, eh?"

"Yeah, I was asked to come in and make a statement. Is Lisa about?" I asked, hoping that I wouldn't have to deal with *Cuntstable* Dick.

"Ah she just popped out for lunch, but PC Handcock, who was with her is available. Said he was expecting you." Kev smiled. "Have a seat, and I'll just go get him."

"Thanks," I said, really not feeling all that thankful as I went and settled in on one of those crappy plastic chairs that were in sets of four, and favoured by hospitals everywhere to make an uncomfortable wait even more uncomfortable.

Thankfully, I didn't have to wait long. One of the doors to the back section of the police station bleeped as its electronic lock disengaged, and it opened, revealing *Cuntstable* Dick.

"Miss Hastings?" He smiled at me, as he opened the door wider and gestured for me to come through.

I got up, pushing from the moulded plastic chair and walked across the linoleum, discoloured in spots from the sunlight that shone through the windows. The old police station needed a little bit of renovation in places, but it was still functional, and hadn't seemed to warrant much attention in regard to maintenance or upkeep of appearances.

I'd only been here once, when I'd been out after my father had attempted to beat me for not keeping the house clean, and I'd been caught roaming the streets with no reasonable explanation as to why I wasn't at home, tucked up 'safe' in bed. The back sections hadn't changed all that much.

Cuntstable Dick lead me to one of the interview rooms, where two cups of tea were waiting.

"I took the liberty of getting you a cup of tea," he smiled, pulling out a seat for me, before he took the one opposite.

"That standard procedure?" I asked, a little snidely.

Dick grinned. "Nope, just thought you might like a cup of tea." He settled in his seat and opened a clipboard with a lined notepad clipped to it

"Uh, okay. Thanks, I guess." I reached for the steaming foam cup and slowly pulled it towards me.

Dick grabbed his and took a sip. "Okay, so in your own words, can you please tell me what happened today?"

He picked up a pen and began to write down the details of the meeting.

I leaned forward, my hands clasping the cup as I began. "I was working my stall at the local Saturday market when I saw this young man in a white shirt reach into a woman's purse and pull out a phone and a wallet. He quickly took the money out of the wallet and dropped it, kicking it under Farmer Trotter's produce stall before moving on. I noticed you and Lisa—"

"PC Smythe," Dick corrected me, scribbling down on the notepad

"Right, PC Smythe…" I said with a touch of ire in my voice at being corrected. "…following him and keeping an eye on things. I continued to work at my stall until you tried to stop the young man, who then turned and fled, running back towards me. I then decided to try and help, don't know why, just did it. So, I walked into his path and tripped him up, allowing you and *PC Smythe* to catch him."

"Okay, and did you see anything else, any other thefts?" he asked, the pen scratching over the lined paper.

"I did see him slip his hand inside someone else's bag and take another phone just before you tried to get him." Dick nodded.

"That was all?" he asked.

"Yep." I picked up my cooling tea and sipped it, leaning back in the chair.

"All right. Let me just read this back to you, and I'll get you to sign and date your statement."

I nodded, listening to him read back what I'd said in my statement as I sipped at my tea. It was sweet and still slightly hot, but that perfect temperature to be enjoyed.

"Sounds about right," I said, finishing my tea.

"Excellent," *Cuntstable* Dick said, sliding the pad over to me, and handing me the pen. My fingers brushed against his as I took the pen, feeling a little jolt of static electricity as I took the metal pen from his fingers. He smiled warmly as I looked up at him, before diverting my full attention to my statement and signing on the dotted line.

"All right, now that's done, I'm pretty sure I owe you a drink." He grinned. "How about I pick you up at seven tonight?"

Ah...so that's your game? I shook my head in bewilderment. "Can't. I have a wedding to shoot this afternoon, and I'll be shooting at the reception till late."

"Raincheck?" he asked, his eyes hopeful.

I sighed. "Listen, I don't know what you're playing at, but I don't think I'm your type of girl." I leaned forward. "Seriously, I'm not sure I like you, you were a real arse to me the first time I met you—" I held up my hand. "I know, I know, you were doing your job." I crossed my arms on the table and leaned over on them. "And yes, you did buy a picture that I had actually thrown out, *and* paid too much for it in my opinion, and then you found me at my weakest, and you still want to take me out for a drink?" I leaned back, leaving my hands on the table, my eyes searching for an answer in the look he was giving me. "I'm damaged goods Di—*Richard*," I said, actually using his proper name felt weird. "What could you possibly want from me?"

"Libby," he said softly. "I like you, you're smart, witty, funny, beautiful. I would love to get to know you better, start out as friends, maybe even see where that goes." He reached forward, a large hand reaching forward tentatively, fingertips caressing my knuckles. "And you're not damaged. You are just, maybe, a little lost. I want to find you."

"Uh…ok-ay…" I said, pulling away. I got up and walked out the door, leaving him alone in the interview room, my mind a maelstrom of thoughts.

He wanted to get to know me better? To *find* me?

What. The. Fuck?

Chapter Fifteen.

The next day went by without sight nor sound of *Cuntstable* Dick. For that, I was kinda glad.

I vegged out on the couch as the photos from the evening before developed in my bathroom-come-darkroom. Several had already developed and had dried. I'd laid them out on the kitchen table and let LP in from outside at about midnight, before I lay down on the sofa again.

I'd been watching some silly soap opera and had drifted off when a sound woke me… The unmistakable sound of a cat in the first stages of throwing up.

I bucked up off the couch, my legs flying upwards, as did my torso, just enough to see over the back of the couch into the kitchen where LP was. The poor boy was hunched over, back arched as he retched, bobbing his head as if he were in a sickly cat mosh pit. The worst part wasn't that I knew he was going to be sick. The worst part was that he was perched atop the kitchen table. Right on top of the beautiful photographs I'd taken of the bride and groom. The ones they'd specifically asked to have ready tomorrow for their bridal breakfast.

I struggled off the couch, my feet thumping on the thinning carpet towards LP in a desperate effort to save the photographs that had already been paid for, with a damned guarantee that the pictures would be delivered to them in the morning. I reached for my poor pussycat just as his mouth opened. I cried out in abject horror as his lips pulled back in a rictus, his jaw opened, showing his sharp little fangs, and curling tongue as stomach acid and congealed feathers erupted from his mouth to splatter all over the photographs of the smiling bride and groom.

"No!!!" I cried out, as I ran from carpet to cheap linoleum. My bare foot squelched in something that felt warm, and disgusting…and reeked of cat vomit.

This wasn't the first of LPs pukes this evening. I skidded in the small pile of puke and landed hard on my arse with a grunt as LP retched once more and then jumped off the table, darting towards the bathroom where he liked to hide behind the toilet or the washing basket if he knew he was in trouble.

"Seriously? Come on!" I bemoaned to the heavens. "Fuck me, not even Mel has this much bad luck." I thought for a moment on that statement. "Okay, maybe she does." I groaned as I sat up, rubbing my butt only to discover it too was smeared with vomit. "Really, LP? Seriously?" I felt my stomach churn at the bits of badly digested blue bird feathers that were stuck to my hand. "Cat. We seriously need to talk about your eating habits." I peeked over the top of the table. "And your opinion on my photography."

I hauled my arse up, ignoring the squishy stuff on the bottom of my foot. I hobbled over to the bathroom and turned on the light. A pair of green eyes looked at me from behind the washing basket. "You do realise I'm going to be really fucking late with this order now, don't you?" I asked him.

I sighed, stripping my clothes and dumping them into the basket. My washing day would have to be bumped up from Tuesday to as soon as the pictures I'd have to develop a second time were dry.

I finished scrubbing the parts of my body that had been in contact with LP's stomach contents before I left the bathroom to clean up the mess he'd made. I wasn't great with cleaning up vomit, especially when parts of it were still identifiable with whatever had been eaten.

I finally finished cleaning up, and disinfecting the kitchen table, the floor and my body. Then I set to work on getting the reprints done. My eyes felt like someone had thrown coarse sand in them and I felt like I needed another shower by the time I was done a few hours later. But I finally had the last of the photographs dried and in their frames, which fortunately, had not been on the table. I carefully placed them in the gift bags that the bride and groom had provided, which also had escaped the vomitus attack from my feline.

I checked my hair and makeup in the mirror beside my front door, before I realised how bloodshot my eyes looked. I groaned, before I headed back to the bathroom where I scrounged for my old friend, Mr Clear Eyes. I sighed softly as the lubricating eye drops did their job, easing the gritty feeling from beneath my eyelids. There was a soft knocking at the door.

"Who the bloody hell could that be?" I wondered to myself.

I opened the door to find Mrs MacDonald, one of my elderly neighbours at my door. The poor old dear was hunched over with arthritis, and osteoporosis, but she had somehow managed to get up the steps from her flat on the ground floor to my one at the second floor. No mean feat for a woman who kept to herself and only left her flat for her doctor's appointments. Realistically, she should be in a home, as her family didn't come around to see her often.

"Good morning, Elizabeth. I'm so terribly sorry to bother you so early, but it seems that Porridge has gotten out," she said in her sweet, little old lady voice. "You haven't seen him, have you?"

Porridge…her blue budgerigar. My mind flashed back to the disgusting mess of congealed *blue* feathers that LP had puked up all over the kitchen floor and dining table.

Oh shite.

"No, I'm sorry Mrs Mac, I haven't seen him. But if I do find him, I'll try to bring him back to you." I promised her.

"Oh, you are such a good young lady." Mrs MacDonald smiled, taking my hands and patting them with affection. I smiled back, though it was so forced that I was afraid I'd break my fucking cheeks.

I closed the door and turned around to see LP smiling at me, the smug little fucker had the audacity to lick his chops before he began to clean a paw so nonchalantly it made me shake my head. "Really, LP? Of all the fucking birds you could have devoured then puked all over the kitchen, you chose Porridge the budgerigar?" I set my hands on my hips and shook my head again.

"What the Fuck?"

Chapter Sixteen.

I was ninety-nine-point-nine percent certain that LP had killed, eaten and then regurgitated Porridge the budgie. So, after I dropped off the photographs to the grateful couple, without their knowledge that they were a second batch. I said my goodbyes to the loved-up and happy couple and then headed to the local pet shop.

My mission: 'Operation Replacement Porridge' was a go.

I entered the pet shop where the chirps and squawks of birds, the yips and howls of puppies and the yowls and cute squeaking mewls of kittens reached my ears. The ice in my heart began to melt a little as a Husky puppy bounced around the little Perspex-box pen they'd placed him in. There wasn't nearly enough room in there for a large puppy, but no-one had bought him yet. He licked the Perspex where I had placed my hand, his little paws scratching to get at me, then he sat on his haunches and howled. If I had the room, and the money, I'd probably have taken home a new pet to terrorise LP.

But, instead, I was here for an entirely different purpose. Regretfully, I left the cute bundle of mischief, and steadfastly ignored the other little babies looking for their forever homes and made my way to the aviary, where the brilliantly coloured feathers of the caged birds awaited me.

"Hi, can I help you?" The young shop assistant came up beside me, her mouth moving like a cow's as she chewed a piece of gum and popped it between her teeth.

"Uh, yeah, my cat decided to make a meal out of my elderly neighbour's budgerigar, and I wanted to get her a replacement," I said, eyeing the birds off. There were some really pretty budgerigars. In a variety of colours from white pied, right through to an almost iridescent lavender.

"Okay, male or female?" the girl asked, putting her hands on her hips in a casual and relaxed manner, as she continued to chew and pop her gum. I kinda sympathised with the chick in *'Chicago'* who killed her husband for popping his gum. That shit was annoying as fuck and would drive anyone to murder.

"I think Porridge was male," I said, racking my brain to remember.

"Right, and what colour were you thinking of?" The girl moved to a section of cages that was marked 'Male Budgerigars'. Her mouth worked again, then seconds later it came *POP!* I shuddered a little.

"Uh…blue.," I said, feeling a slight wave of nausea come over me as I recalled the blue feathers that LP had brought up. I was getting a little bit irritated at the amount of questions the girl was asking, though she was trying to be helpful. My lack of sleep and lack of food was making me one cranky arse bitch.

"Okay, juvenile or mature?" she asked. *Chew-squish, chew-squish, chew-squish, POP!*

"Look, I just want a fucking blue budgerigar. One that goes chirp-fucking-chirp, and that my fucking cat won't eat and then puke up all over my flat." I stared daggers at her. "Is that too much to fucking ask, or are you going to continue to chew and pop that fucking gum in my face all morning?" I had raised my voice, feeling like I wanted to explode. All the animals in the store were deathly quiet as soon as I had finished.

"Ahem, is there a problem here?" The gruff voice of a man entered my tired and grumpy mind. I looked up. The gum-popping girl had backed away and a burly, fat man stood before me, arms crossed and an unimpressed look on his face. I dared a look at his name badge. 'Larry – Store Manager'. Just fucking great.

"I just want a blue budgerigar." I sighed. "Look, I'm sorry, I have had a very stressful night, which included my cat eating my neighbours pet bird, then vomiting its remains up all over my kitchen, destroying some work I'd laid out on the table, and I have barely slept at all trying to get it finished for my client by this morning. I just want to replace the poor woman's fucking bird and get it home to her, so I can go to bed and get some sleep."

"We can't help you. We have no birds for you."

"But you've got fucking blue budgerigars right there," I said, indicating to the cage filled with the little blue fuckers who all eyed me with suspicious beady little eyes.

"Not for you, we don't. I'm going to have to ask you to leave." He pointed to the door.

"You're fucking kidding me, right? I'm wanting to buy a fucking bird from you, and you're not going to let me?"

"That's exactly right, now get the hell out of my shop!" Behind him, the girl popped her gum with a smirk. I turned and stormed out of the shop, the animals started their noisy calls behind me.

"Arsehole." I grumped, turning to flip him the bird before I turned and stormed out. Three steps later, and not watching where I was going, I collided with a tight, muscled chest.

"Oof!" I grunted, butt-smacking the pavement. With all the mistreatment, my arse was going to be black and blue

"Hey, Everything okay?" Robbie asked, helping me up.

"Fuck no." I sighed. Shaking my head as I got to my feet. Robbie, Mel's brother was so kind, a gentle soul, and a gentleman, I would have loved to have him as a boyfriend, if I were his type. He was more Zane's type, and from what I knew, especially from 'Uncle' Leo's grumbling about it more two years after the 'event', Robbie and Zane were no longer allowed in the tool shed alone together.

"Come on, Mel's in town, she was going to call in to see you on her way out. Let's go get a cup of tea with her, and you can spill."

"Fuck, that would be just what I need right now."

"You certainly look like you need it. You look like shite, old duck."

Robbie put an arm around my shoulders and we headed to Rosie's café, a place where we had hung out many times, and our usual table was often available. The one with the crude pictures of cocks drawn on the cracked vinyl. Rosie had left them there in honour of the 'artist', Ollie, a high school friend who was killed in a car accident. I smirked, running a hand over the cracked vinyl, my painted fingernails tracing one of the black lines of the cocks, which included hairy balls, and a few drops of cum dripping from the exaggerated tip.

Mel waddled in from out back where the bathrooms were and sat down with a slight wince.

"Hey Mummy, how's things? Ready to pop?" I smiled.

"Yeah, been feeling a bit weird all day, hardly slept last night, I have a very sore back," she said, reaching behind awkwardly to rub at the sore spot.

"Should you be out and about?" I asked.

"I'm fine," Mel said, as Rosie came over and placed a teapot and three cups in front of us.

"Decaf for you, love." She smiled, placing a smaller pot down in front of her.

"Thanks Rosie." Mel smiled as Rosie placed a hand on Mel's shoulder.

"All right, so what's wrong with you? Looks like your cat died," Mel said, pouring her tea. I noticed her wince a little bit as she lifted the teapot.

"I got that," Robbie said as he reached over and took the pot from Mel.

"Well, you're not far from the mark," I muttered, relaying everything that had happened.

Mel gave us a funny look. "I think I need to…" Her mouth dropped open as the sound of liquid splashing on the floor silenced the café.

"I…oh shit… Uhm… Robbie, can you call Adam…"

"He's in Scotland, Mel," Robbie said, giving his sister a strange look.

"I know, dear brother," Mel said, her face going pale. "I think my water just broke, is all, and I think my husband would LOVE TO KNOW THAT!" She near shouted the last.

"Oh my God! Mel!" I gasped my heart pounding. "Robbie fucking go and call Adam!"

"Right now?" Robbie asked, incredulously. "You're having the baby now?"

"Yes, right fucking now!" Mel gasped as a contraction hit she looked up, her eyes flashing as if possessed by some demonic spirit as she reached out and grabbed Robbie's shirtfront. "In fact, if you don't fucking hurry up and get him here, I might just drop this baby right here, right now!"

"Okay! Okay, I'm dialling now!" Robbie said, pushing away from his sister, I pushed Robbie out of the way and went to Mel's side. "Okay Slut, we're going to take a nice, deep breath, then we're going to get the ambulance here to get you to the hospital, okay?"

"Please, hurry." Mel gasped, her hands clutching her swollen belly, as if that might stop her from giving birth. I quickly dialled the emergency services.

"Hi, my friend is in labour, we need an ambulance right away," I said, once the operator picked up.

"What's your location?"

"Rosie's Café, King Street, Miltonford."

"Okay, you might have a bit of a wait, there was a large accident on the motorway, we can get you an ambulance, but it's about an hour or so away."

"You're fucking kidding me, right? An hour? She's having this baby now!"

I'm sorry Miss, I know you're under a bit of stress right now. But that's all we have, I'm afraid. You may have to get your friend to the hospital yourself, or see if there's a local police officer available to escort you under lights and sirens."

I looked up as she said that, Mel whimpering as another contraction hit, they were coming quick. A familiar figure was writing out a parking ticket as Robbie was talking on his phone, animatedly, his body language panicked. I knew what I had to do. My pride was swallowed.

"Mel, I'll be right back!" I said, as I hung up the call to the emergency services.

They say pride goes before a fall, and my friend needed my help, and the help of the man who was writing that parking ticket.

What the fuck.

Chapter Seventeen.

"RICHARD!" I cried as I ran out the door of Rosie's Café, the little tin bells tinkling as the door swung. Robbie shrieked like a little girl as I burst out the door. *Cuntstable* Dick turned, his face surprised to see me in my flustered and exhausted state. "I need your help! Mel's gone into labour, we need to get to the hospital now!"

I stopped just short of bowling him over. He put his hands on my arms to steady me, and I swear I fucking *swooned* just for a moment in his grip.

"Did you call an ambulance?" he asked, tucking his ticket book back in his Batman-like utility belt.

"Tried, but there's been an accident on the motorway. The closest ambulance is about an hour away. If you can get us to the hospital, I'll be forever grateful. I'll take you out for coffee, dinner, drinks, dancing whatever you want!" I waved my hands like a madwoman.

"Okay, go back to Mel and wait for me. I'll bring the car around. Tell her to keep as calm as she can, we'll be there in no time," he said, placing a reassuring hand on my arm.

"Thank-you!" I said, tears threatening to break free in gratitude.

I turned and bolted back into the café. Robbie was there, holding Mel's hands and wincing when she gripped him with a vice-like grip.

"Did you call your parents?" I asked. Robbie shook his head. "Go do that, Can Leo bring them in?"

"No, I got the van, Dad will need it to get to the hospital."

After his stroke, Mel and Robbie's Dad, Gilbert Whittaker. had lost most of the mobility in his legs, had had been confined to a wheelchair. Robbie had their Nursery's work van modified to accommodate their father's change in mobility, and it was their primary way of getting him around when he needed to leave home, or the nursery.

"Call them, then go get them. They'll want to be here, oh and Mrs Del Rosa too!"

I knew the family well enough that everyone would want to be nearby for the birth of Mel and Adam's first baby. Robbie nodded and ran out the door like the hounds of hell were on his arse. I turned back to Mel, Rosie had come over and was helping her to settle back in the bench seat covered in cocks.

"Libby… I can't do this…" She whimpered, her face showing how scared she was.

"It's going to be okay, Mel. Your baby is ready to come and meet you," I said, feeling the sting of tears prickling behind my eyes.

"What if something goes wrong?" She sobbed, whimpering as her body tensed with another contraction. Rosie had brought out some tea towels and had laid them under Mel to help soak up some of the fluid.

"You'll be fine, love." Rosie smiled, patting Mel's hand.

"I want Adam, and my Mum!" Mel sobbed.

"I know skank, they're on their way," I soothed, looking up over the table to see the flashing blue lights heralding our chariot had arrived.

"Hi Mel," Richard said, striding in like a hero, and yes, I guess he was. "I'm PC Handcock, a friend of Libby's here. I've got a special ride for you, ever been in the back of a police car?" He grinned.

Mel choked out a half-sob-half laugh. "Nope, but I'm sure the Paps will love that."

"Yeah." I agreed, "Just remember, I got the rights to the official photos of you and your new bub." I grinned.

"All about the publicity, isn't it?" Mel huffed through another contraction.

"Your contractions seem to be coming a bit quick. We need to get you to the hospital now, else Rosie will have something else to have this bench be famous for." Dick said. "Let's get you up, okay. This is going to be nice and slow, a bit of a shuffle to the car. I'll be on one side, and Libby on the other, okay? Rosie, can you get the back door to my car please?" Dick asked Rosie, who nodded and ran to the door of her café, holding it open for us to help Mel out and to the car.

"Okay, Mel we're going to turn you around and you'll sit back in the back seat of my car, then I need you to do a backwards butt-shuffle to the other side so Libby can sit in the back with you." Mel nodded, whining with the pain as another bloody contraction hit. "Okay let's get you in."

Dick and I helped Mel into the back seat, she did her best to shove herself backwards, gasping as her body complained with the process of labour.

"You're doing great, Mel," I said as Dick shut the doors and got in the front.

"Fuck you, just fuck you." She huffed.

"Atta girl." I grinned, letting her grip my hands. Her response was a pain-filled wail broken by a heartfelt sob and plea for Adam.

"He's on the way Mel, I promise. It won't take him long, he's had a private jet on standby just for this occasion, you know that. He'll be here in about an hour, okay?"

"This is taking forever!" Mel whined as we rounded a corner, the lights and sirens blaring.

"If it's any consolation, Mel, my sister took three days with her first baby." Richard offered, *Dick.*

"Not helping, Dick!" I grumbled.

"Sorry!" He chuckled.

He pulled up outside the hospital's emergency ward entrance. Mel huffed and puffed like the big bad wolf in the back seat, while Dick ran inside to get a wheelchair, or gurney, or some sort of mobility device to get Mel's pregnant arse inside.

"That's it Mel, you got some sexy doctors and nurses coming to help ease your pain."

"Yeah, how about a sexy PC to help ease yours?" Mel said with a sweaty smile.

"Don't you go playing matchmaker on me girl." I grinned, turning to open the door, and finding that Dick was on the other side already pulling it open. Two orderlies waited with a wheelchair, along with a nurse and a doctor.

"Hello Mrs Jacobs. Looks like we're ready for you to have this baby, eh?" the doctor said with a grin. I recognised him as Mel's OB/GYN.

I scrambled out and let the men help Mel into the chair. Her hand reached out for mine and I grasped it. "I'll be right in, Mel," I said, my eyes catching Dick's.

Mel's fingers stayed touching mine until the distance they took her in the wheelchair became so great that her fingers slipped from mine.

I watched her as she was pushed through the sliding doors and ran a hand through my short hair. I turned to face Dick... *Richard.*

"Richard, thank you..." I said, and without thinking. I leaned forward and kissed him.

Right. On. The. Mouth.

What.

The.

FUCK?

Chapter Eighteen.

Tiny little fingers curled around my index finger as the baby boy snuggled against the blanket the nurses had swaddled him in. The cheeky little bugger had waited until his panting and exhausted father was seconds inside the door before he made his grand entrance, screaming blue murder and covered in blood and gunk.

Adam was slumped, exhausted on an easychair, soft snores coming from him, while Mel dozed a little from the medication they'd given her. They'd had to cut her a little bit to get the boy in my arms out, as he had a big head and broad shoulders on him. Considering he was his father's son, it wasn't surprising. But for poor Mel, it was an ordeal.

I looked down at my beautiful Godson's face and wondered what my own baby might have looked like. He grumbled a little in my arms, becoming restless—until I gently rocked him in my arms and quietly shushed him, leaning down to press a kiss against his warm forehead, breathing in the scent of a newborn.

Mel's room had been a constant revolving door of visitors. The vast number of flowers, stuffed toys and blue balloons that decorated the place made the room feel like a florist shop and not a private room in a hospital.

There was a soft knock on the door. I looked up as it opened. Richard entered, carrying a bunch of flowers and a small blue-wrapped parcel.

"Hey, that's a good look on you." He smiled.

I couldn't help it, I felt the tears rolling down my cheeks.

"Yeah, he's beautiful," I said, as Richard came closer, placing the flowers on a rare empty space, and keeping hold of the blue-wrapped box.

"PC Handcock," Mel said softly from the bed, her voice tinged with tiredness.

"Hello Mrs Jacobs. Congratulations, he's a fine-looking lad." He smiled.

Mel raised her arms, gesturing for me to return the slumbering bundle. I did, with a little reluctance. I wanted to hold him forever, I knew I'd be a big part of his life, but he needed his Mummy bonding time. Time my own bitch of a mother obviously never had with me.

Adam yawned and stretched in the chair, slowly coming awake.

"Adam, this is the officer who drove us to the hospital." I introduced him.

"Wow, I can't thank you enough for taking care of my family."

"Think nothing of it. It was Libby here who told me what was happening. Unfortunately, we didn't have enough ambulances to come pick her up, what with a seven-car pileup on the motorway."

"Damn, hope nobody was hurt."

"Unfortunately, there was one fatality. But we believe he had a heart attack while driving, which caused the accident, so it was believed he passed before the crash."

"Wow, that's not good."

"No, but we at least got your wife to the hospital in time." He grinned. "Here, this is for your son." He handed the blue-wrapped parcel. "From the Miltonford Police Department." He turned and picked up the flowers from their spot. "And this is for you, Mrs Jacobs."

"Mel, please call me Mel." Mel grinned, taking the flowers, inhaling their sweet fragrance and placing them beside her. "They're lovely."

The sound of wrapping paper being torn apart directed our attention to Adam, who was ripping the carefully wrapped blue paper to shreds like a big kid. "Oh wow, a Police Bear!"

"That is an official Bobby Bear," Richard said, nodding to the boxed bear.

"That is so cool. He even has a little ID badge!" Adam was transfixed with the stuffed bear, decked out in full police uniform.

"I think you might need another bear," I said to Richard, leaning in and shoulder bumping him slightly. He turned his head to me and grinned. "Maybe." He cleared his throat. "Anyway, I was wondering if I could steal Libby away for a little bit? I believe she owes me a coffee."

"I do?" I asked, innocently.

"I believe your exact words were, 'coffee, dinner, drinks dancing or anything.'" He grinned, before he leaned in and whispered. 'I'll take all five, if the offer is still there."

I looked at him as he leaned back and smiled warmly at me.

"Okay," I agreed. "Coffee." I turned to Mel, who was smiling knowingly, while Adam was looking at the back of the Bobby Bear's box.

"Hey, babe, the profits of each bear sold goes to the families of police officers who've lost their lives in the line of duty," Adam said with a hint of awe in his voice.

"Go, he'll be going over that for hours, then the next thing you'll know, we'll have a collection of Police bears from all over the world." Mel shooed us out the door. I smiled at her, catching a sly wink as I closed the door behind us, leaving me alone in the corridor with *Cunt*—I mean Richard.

"So…" I said, suddenly at a loss as to what to say.

"Coffee…" He grinned, offering his hand to me.

"I thought you only drank tea?" I asked, taking his hand and suppressing a delighted shiver as his fingers wrapped around mine in a somewhat possessive but protective grip.

"I do, but on occasion, I do drink coffee, but I think you're right. Tea it is."

He led me out of the maternity ward and out of the hospital, where his car waited. Like a gentleman, he opened the door and helped me in, waiting until I was seated and buckled in before he closed the door and went to the driver's side.

"Any place in particular you'd like to go for tea?" he asked, starting up the car.

"Rosie's is good, and I think she'd want to know Mel is okay.

"Rosie's, it is." He grinned and pulled out of the hospital parking lot. We drove in a somewhat comfortable silence, though I was a little bit nervous, well, fucking antsy would probably be closer to the truth. His aftershave danced through my senses, and the warmth he exuded was comforting after a long, and stressful twenty-four hours at the hospital.

"So, I take it everything went well?" Richard asked.

"Yes, though not without a few funny incidents that we'll no doubt be telling the boy about when he's older," I chuckled, as I recounted the events in the delivery room and maternity ward.

Mel's labour had been hard on everyone, but obviously most of all, on Mel. Her parents had come in after the as-yet unnamed boy was born, Robbie rushing in with his father's wheelchair, minus his father…whom had been left in the van due to Robbie's panicking mind going completely blank. He'd received an ear bashing from his mother, when she'd calmly wheeled their father in a borrowed wheelchair through the maternity waiting room doors to find Robbie standing with his father's empty wheelchair.

Richard chuckled as he pulled to a stop outside Rosie's. He got out of the car and rushed to the passenger side as I opened the door to get out. His hand offered to help me up, and I took it. I'd never been treated in such a genteel manner before. It was fucking odd.

He opened the door to Rosie's for me, and led me to a small table, set out of the way and secluded from everyone. Rosie had set it up for two, with a clean tablecloth and one of the nicest china sets I'd seen on her table.

"What's all this?" I asked, looking at him.

"Tea, for two." Richard smiled, placing a hand on the small of my back and guiding me towards the table.

"Right…" I gave him a quizzical look, but he just smirked. The cocky bastard.

He settled me down, pulling out my chair for me, more behaviour I wasn't used to, before he settled in across from me.

Rosie came and poured our tea for us. Richard just kept a level and easy gaze on me. It felt uncomfortable for the first few seconds, but soon, it felt…*normal*. Natural, wanted. I felt my heart beating a little bit faster as I stirred sugar and milk into my tea.

"So, tell me a little about yourself, Richard? Why did you come to Miltonford?"

"Well, I was so good at my job in London, they asked me to come here. I have an excellent arrest record, but they felt I was taking too much away from everyone else."

"Like the film, *Hot Fuzz*?" I asked.

He chuckled. "Yeah, kinda like that, but at least, I don't think there's a secret society of folk in the village happy to kill people to keep their village the way they want it."

I leaned forward conspiratorially. "How do you know there's not?" I asked with a sly grin.

He snorted, his tea dribbling down his front. "Smart arse." He grabbed a napkin and dabbed it down the damp spots where he'd spilled his tea.

There was a sudden fluttering noise, sounding suspiciously like wings and a disgruntled chirping noise coming from beneath the table.

"What was that?" I asked, frowning a little.

"That?" Richard smirked. "Well, a little birdy told me you were trying to replace a little birdy…"

He reached under the table and pulled out a small cage with a blue bow on the top. Within sat a little male budgerigar, his plumage a pretty sapphire-like blue. He eyed me with beady little eyes.

"What the fuck?"

Chapter Nineteen

After Rosie's, Richard had suggested we take Porridge the Second to his new home. I was more than happy to have him accompany me, mainly because I was worried that Mrs Mac might get so upset she'd have a fucking coronary.

Thankfully, she was an understanding lovely lady.

I knocked on her door a little hesitant about the possible confrontation. Richard stood behind me, holding the cage with a little blue bow tied to the handle.

"Hi Mrs Mac, I've got some news about Porridge," I said, smiling a little sadly.

"Oh! Did you find him?" Her eyes brightened with hope.

"Ah…sort of," I said.

"Oh, that's wonderful!" She beamed. "But where are my manners? Please, come in and let's have a cup of tea. You can set Porridge down on the table there. I'm so glad he's home."

I followed her in, Richard closed the door behind us. Her little flat was cosy, music played from the fifties on a CD player, and the entire pace smelled like old lady and tea.

Little knick-knacks were carefully arranged on the many bookshelves that lined her walls, along with a collection of Harlequin and Mills and Boon romance books the likes of which I'd never seen. It was obvious that Mrs Mac was a very lonely woman.

Richard set the bird cage down on the coffee table. The little blue feathered fucker flapped and fluttered around, squawking with indignation at being shuffled around in such a way. We both settled on the loveseat, leaving the worn-looking armchair, that was obviously Mrs Mac's favourite spot, for her to take. While she bustled about in the kitchen, Richard looked at me and smiled. He placed a warm hand on my knee and gently rubbed his hand back and forth. I felt little tingles shooting up and down my leg. I slowly placed my hand over his, my fingers intertwining with his.

"Here we go, dearies," she said, settling a tray on the coffee table with trembling hands that made the teacups rattle on their saucers.

I pulled my hand away from his, almost feeling like I'd been caught with my hand in the biscuit tin, especially with the way my cheeks flushed.

Mrs Mac settled down in the armchair and looked at the bird. "Wait… That's not porridge…" she said softly.

"Mrs Mac, I can explain," I said, shifting forward on the couch. "I think my cat got him. I let him in the other night, and he was sick in the early morning. There were blue feathers, and I think he might have eaten Porridge." I sighed.

"I went to buy you a new bird, but I hadn't had much sleep, and I was under a lot of stress, and got angry with the girl at the pet shop, so they threw me out. Then, my best friend went into labour while we were having tea at Rosie's, so, we had to rush her to the hospital, and then Richard here," I turned and smiled at him, my body warming when he smiled back, "who is one of the local police officers, came by the hospital, took me out, and revealed that he knew what had happened. He'd gotten a replacement bird." I finished in a rush

"Oh, he's a sweetie," Mrs MacDonald said as she looked into the cage.

"Again, I'm so very sorry about Porridge, Mrs Mac."

"It's nature, my dear. Cats will eat birds, and though Porridge will always have a place in my heart, he was an older budgerigar, probably not far from falling off the perch himself."

I sat on her floral loveseat, Richard beside me as we nursed fine china cups of tea in our hands. We chatted a little while longer, until Mrs Mac finished her tea and took the cage in her hands. She busied herself with setting the bird on the bench beside the forlorn-looking empty cage which once housed Porridge, all the while cooing at the bird in the cage.

"Well, I think it's time to go," I said, pushing up from the loveseat, Richard following my lead.

Mrs Mac turned and smiled. "Thank you, my dears. Again, I'm so thankful you told me about Porridge, and thank you for bringing me my new little friend."

"That's quite all right, Mrs MacDonald," Richard said. He smiled as the sweet little old lady wrapped her arms in a motherly hug, completely dwarfed by Richard. I couldn't help but smile.

"And you too, Elizabeth, dear." She pulled me in to the hug, I smiled as I felt Richard's hand slide along the small of my back, his pinkie fingers dangerously close to the top of my arse.

"Now, you two make such a lovely couple," she said, pulling back.

Richard still had his arm around me, and pulled me against his side as soon as Mrs Mac was clear. I didn't correct her, but I knew there was really no hope of us being together, despite the fact that Richard wanted to 'get to know me better'. I was still too broken inside, unfixable.

We left Mrs Mac's place, and headed up the stairs to my flat.

"Well," I said, unlocking my door. "I can't thank you enough for everything, Richard."

"I'm glad to see I've been promoted from 'Cuntstable Dick to Richard, but you can call me Richard, if you like, Libby." He smiled, even my name on his lips gave me tingles of illicit pleasure.

I ducked my head, lowering my eyes in embarrassment. "Well, yeah. Look, I am sorry about that, but you really pissed me off when we first met." For whatever reason, I couldn't meet his intense gaze.

"I understand," Richard said. "But, I'm glad you've forgiven me, it means I can do this…"

He reached under my chin and lifted it up, so I was looking into his eyes. They mesmerised me, and made my body tingle with his touch and anticipation of what he was about to do—yeah, I know, I was thinking some sappy fucking shit that was more appropriate in Mrs Mac's bodice-ripper collection.

He leaned forward and pressed his lips against mine. I smelled him, felt the scratch stubble of his chin and upper lip abrading against my skin like sandpaper, the soft, but slightly insistent press of his tongue against my lips, asking me to invite it in for a cup of tea, or a roll around my mouth. I parted my lips just enough for him to get a peek in. Richard put his arms around me, pulling me flush against his body. I couldn't help myself, I fucking put my arms around him too. I felt him pulling away, part of me didn't want him to go, but the insistent ringing of his phone broke through the haze of lust that was roaring through my ears.

"Damn, I'm sorry Libby. I have to get this," he said with a regretful smile as he pulled his phone from his pocket and stepped away.

"That's fine," I murmured, my lips humming from that *fucking* kiss!

If I somehow fell down the stairs and broke my neck, at least I'd die a happy girl…well kinda happy. I'd felt the man's body while he was pressed up against me, and fuck me sideways with a rusty mace, it made my lady bits cry out like there had been a disturbance in the Force.

I needed to get laid, and something told me that this fine specimen who stood at the end of the walkway talking animatedly was the only one who could scratch that itch.

Relationship? Nah.

Beast with two backs? Bit of the old in-out? A bit of how's your father? Fuck yes!

I waited by my door, wondering if I should bang him over the head and go cavewoman style on him, drag him into my flat and have my wicked, wicked way with him. He ended his call and sighed, before he walked back to me.

"Come in for a cuppa?" I offered, giving him a sultry smile.

"Sorry Libby, I can't something has come up, I really wish it hadn't, but I have to go," he said, regret showing in his eyes.

"Oh, okay, that's fine," I said softly, feeling the sting of rejection.

"It's not like that, I promise," he said, reaching up to caress my face with his warm hands. He leaned forward and gently pressed his lips to mine, reminding me that he really wanted to be with me.

"I'll see you next weekend at the ball, right?" he asked, breaking the kiss.

"Sure," I said, with a smile that didn't quite feel genuine. I still felt like I was getting rejected.

"Save me a dance, okay?" He grinned then pulled away from me.

He walked past a very stunned looking Zane, who had witnessed the kiss. I slumped against the door frame as Richard… *Dick* headed to his car. There was definitely something going on that I couldn't put my finger on just yet.

Zane's face, however was priceless, I could see the shock and surprise written all over it with the perfect 'o' on his lips. "Girl…" he said, giving me one of his 'spill it' looks.

"What the fuck?"

Chapter Twenty.

"Okay, so just relax, lean down a little bit, and give me a soft pout," I said, peering through the lens of the camera. "Right there, that's perfect." I snapped a few shots on the old SLR before switching to the digital camera and taking a few more.

Zane was posing perfectly, and the shots were going to look great in both our portfolios. I was slowly building up my own for consideration in a few upcoming London fashion shows that Danny had suggested I put in for. He had a couple of mates in London who were fashion photographers, and he knew it was one of my dreams to work as a runway photographer. But now, I was in the beautiful gardens at the Whittaker Nursery and Café, with Zane stealing the limelight, as we took shot after shot, after shot of him posing and primping. He'd been working out a little in Adam's home gym while staying with Mel and Adam. I was going to go there later and work with them on the 'official' baby photos with them and baby Aaron.

They had finally decided on naming him after Adam's twin brother, who had died after losing his battle with an aggressive form of Leukaemia. Adam's biological mum, Mrs Del Rosa was visiting her new grandson, which, of course, meant Uncle Leo was visiting Mrs Del Rosa.

They were the worst kept secret.

"So, what time is the policeman's ball?" Zane asked.

"This evening, starting around seven," I said, taking a few natural snaps of him.

"You going to wear something dressy?" He settled down on the white concrete edge of a medium sized fountain. Mel had designed the entire garden and café complex that had brought their family's business up a notch.

"You mean like a dress?" I asked.

"Sure." He smirked, running his hands through the water. I quickly took a few snaps.

"Don't have one."

It was true, I really didn't I was going to wear some fancy dress pants and a nice top.

"Oh hell, no." Zane pulled his hand out of the water, shaking the droplets free. "We are going to go and raid Mel's wardrobe." He eyed me up and down. "I think you'll fit into some of her gowns."

"I can't do that! Do you even know how expensive her things are?" I saved the last pictures on the digital camera and began to pack away my gear.

"Mel will be fine with it, besides, she's married to 'Mr Rich and Famous.' He'll buy her more shit."

"Fucking hell Zane. I don't want to wear a gown."

"What? You don't want ease of access for Mr Hottie McCopper?" Zane said with a wink.

"It's not that!" *It's totally that!* "I'll be working, and besides, I don't think he's really all that into me." I carefully placed my digital camera into the bag and zipped it up.

"Uh...*excuse me?*" Zane shook his head in utter disgust. "Honey, even a blind man could see he was into you. The way he was playing tonsil hockey with you. Hell, I'd have me a piece of that if I thought he swung my way!" Zane moved up beside me and placed a hand on my shoulder. "Honey, trust me. He wants you. And after I'm done with you, he'll be all over you like a fat kid on a cupcake." He smirked.

Fucker.

"Fine." I relented. "Let's go get this gorgeous baby shoot done, then you can have at me."

"Squee!" Zane giggled.

"Uh, did you fucking 'squee' just then?"

"Maybe." He giggled.

"Ugh really?"

"Come on, sweet cheeks." Zane picked up my camera bags and *thankfully* was careful in how he handled the delicate equipment. "Let's get you sexified, after the cute widdle baby pictures!" He imitated a babying voice at the last. I rolled my eyes.

"Fucking wanker," I muttered as we walked through the gardens and up to the security gate at the back that led to Mel's place.

An hour, and hundreds of photographs later, and Aaron was getting fussy. I'd tried to keep the flash off as long as possible to keep his little eyes safe, but there was only so much I could do. I could see he was getting tired, and Mel was fussing almost as much as her baby.

Zane came up behind me as I was packing my cameras away for the second time.

"Okay, so, let's get our Cinderella ready for the ball."

"What ball?" Mel asked, as she rocked Aaron in her arms, the little mite making gurgling and cooing noises as he started to drift off.

"The policeman's ball," Zane said with a wink.

"Actually, it's the fireman's, paramedic's and policeman's ball," I said,

"Do you have a dress?" Mel asked.

I shook my head in the negative, as Zane came up behind me and placed his hands on my shoulders, before ducking his head beside mine and pressing his cheek against mine.

"I was going to ask you if Libby could borrow one of your gowns?" Zane asked with a raised eyebrow.

"Of course, hmm...maybe the sapphire blue one?" Mel suggested.

"Exactly the one I was thinking of." Zane grinned.

"What sapphire one?" I asked. Zane had already literally run out of the nursery where the majority of the photos had been taken. He dashed back in carrying a garment bag. With a flourish, he unzipped it, revealing the floor length slim gown that would undoubtedly hug my skinny-as-fuck body.

"Wow, that's…amazing," I said. Zane nodded with a wicked grin.

"Now, how are you with grooming down below?" Zane asked, holding up a home-waxing kit.

"Uh…?"

"Are you 'bare down there'?" he grinned.

"What the fuck?"

Chapter Twenty-One.

I could have fucking killed Zane. His 'home waxing kit' was more like a 'home fucking TORTURE kit.'

I smiled at the handsome men as they moved around the local church hall, tuxedoes and bow ties and cummerbunds—oh my! My cameras clicked and flashed as I took each photograph, ignoring the burning pain of my hair follicles around my thighs, and up between them, having been ripped out. I had to get help with my underarms, Zane had obliged, and nearly fainted when he saw the little pinpricks of blood.

Wasn't my bloody fault that I'd never waxed before.

I watched from the sidelines as the attendants of the Miltonford Emergency Services Ball swung their dance partners around the dance floor to old timey songs.

I had a glass of wine in one hand and my digital camera in the other. I'd also set up a photography area in one of the small rooms in the hall. With the backdrop and most of the portrait gear set up, I'd already had one session early on when everyone was arriving, but had been asked for a second session later on by the organisers.

I took a sip of my wine just as a hand ran over my back and around my waist.

"Good evening, Miss Hastings. Might I say, you look particularly gorgeous tonight." Dick's voice drifted over the music against my ear, his breath warm against my cheek. I swallowed the wine in my mouth before I turned to him.

"Good evening, Mr Handcock," I said, turning to face him.

He kept his hand on my waist as I spun, bringing his other hand to pluck my glass from my hand.

"Will you dance with me?" he asked, his eyes hopeful.

"I…" I held up my camera. "I am kinda working right now," I said, using my job as an excuse.

"That's okay, I think you can do with a break." He grinned, taking my camera out of my hand and placing it beside my glass.

"What if someone steals it?"

"In a room full of cops?" He chuckled. "Not likely," he said, guiding me to the parquetry of the church hall's floor where other couples were dancing closely to their partners.

He swung me around to face him once more, my body pulled against his, my heart starting to beat faster in my chest at the closeness of him, his scent, his *maleness*. My stripped bare pink bits tingled in a good way, not the stinging aching sensation of total and utter follicle distress.

I sighed as he took my hand and began to lead me around the dancefloor.

"I've been thinking about that kiss," he murmured against my ear.

"Oh? What kiss?" I asked, feigning innocence.

"You don't remember? That scorching as fuck kiss we shared at your apartment?"

I felt naughty, and daring as fuck. I shook my head. "Nope." I leaned forward and pressed my lips to the shell of his ear. "You might have to remind me." I leaned back and looked at him, the heat of lust smouldering in his eyes as he grinned like a schoolboy.

Richard leaned forward, nuzzling his nose against mine at first, rubbing the tip down the side before his lips met mine. I parted my lips at the insistence of his tongue, letting him in, breathing in the scent of his cologne as his mouth ravaged mine on the dancefloor. I felt everything in my body respond to him. I felt his movements stiffen a little bit, and something else in his pants stiffened too. I moved against him, working a little 'dirty dancing' of my own into the innocent-looking waltz we were supposed to be doing.

"Libby." He broke his kiss, groaning against my neck as I slid my thigh forward, rubbing against his crotch. "Oh fuck, if you don't stop, I'm going to have to take you off the dancefloor to somewhere more private."

I smirked, rubbing again.

He groaned, his hands tightening on my body. "That's it, you asked for it," he grunted, gripping my hand and leading me from the dancefloor.

I snagged my digital camera as we passed the table it rested on. He walked past other officers and people who called out greetings to him, nodding or grunting a greeting like a caveman as he pulled me through the hall. Most of the rooms were locked, and his agitation became apparent. He whirled on me, pulling me against his body before he kissed me madly again.

"Fuck… I need to find somewhere quiet and make love to you Libby, this is killing me." He moved his lips to my neck, kissing, licking and nipping the sensitive flesh there.

I breathed hard, wanting the same thing… "I have a room…my camera gear is in there…" I gasped as he bit a little harder on my neck, before softly licking the mark. "We can lock the door, and if we're quiet, we won't be disturbed."

"Let's do it." He smiled, breathing hard and heavy.

"Okay," I said, my words breathy as my chest heaved with the need to take in as much air as possible in preparing my body for what it so desperately needed… *Sex and lots of it!*

I led him to the door and unlocked it, letting him in, with a surreptitious look around the hall. Everyone was minding their own business, dancing, drinking, hob-knobbing, all ignored us as we slipped into the room.

No sooner had I locked the door, then Richard was on me, his hands sliding over the bodice of my dress, slipping around my back until nimble fingers found the hidden zipper. Each tooth that was freed from the zip vibrated down my back right to my needy core. I let the dress fall from my body, getting caught at the widening of my hips. The cold air caressed the swells of my breasts.

I felt Richard's lips press against my shoulder, fingers trebling as they caressed the lines of scars that I'd ever revealed to anyone else… "Oh, baby… Who did this to you?"

I quickly pulled the dress up, back over my naked chest, I turned, trying to hide the shame of my messed-up childhood, the evidence still visible so many years later.

Oh shit.

I'd forgotten about the scars my father had left me… what the fuck was I going to say?

What. The. Fuck?

Chapter Twenty-Two.

"I…" I stopped, unable to formulate any kind of fucking articulate sound. The sensual heat that had suffused my body only moments ago was flushed away with cold dread. I could feel the rejection now, even before he voiced it. I was prepared for the pity, the disgust, the rejection, I wasn't prepared for his anger.

"Who fucking did this to you?" He pulled me into his arms, ignoring my weak attempts to push him away. He pulled me back against him. "Shh… It's okay sweetheart. I got you." He held me as I began to softly cry. We both sank down to the floor together, the warmth of his body against the chill of the air conditioning that pumped through the vents in the ceiling kept me from shivering with cold.

"I understand if you don't want me… I get it," I said, feeling broken. Just another victory for the monsters in my head, and those who were dead and buried, yet still haunted me through their actions in the past.

"I never said I didn't want you, and this changes nothing. I still want you, and I hope you want me too," he said softly, his hand stroking up and down my bare back, fingers sliding over the bumps and lines of my back, fingertips tracing the roadmap of scars that adorned my skin. "When you are ready to, you'll tell me who did this to you, then, we'll deal with them, I promise."

"It's too late, they're dead already."

"Who?"

"My parents," I said, my voice thick.

"Your parents did this to you?" he asked, surprise and anger in his voice.

I nodded, sniffling, and knew that my makeup, so carefully applied by Zane, was now a total disaster zone. "Yeah, my fucking parents. Mother and father of the fucking year. Even when I was really little, they kept telling me how they never wanted me, then as I got older, it turned physical."

"Were you ever…" He paused, as if trying to find the right words. I knew what he was asking, if I'd been sexually abused by my parents.

I shook my head. "No, never got to that, thank fuck. If it had, I'd have fucking killed them both," I said with absolute certainty.

Richard let me cry it out. Speaking softly to me, giving me words of encouragement as I told him of my childhood, the beatings, the verbal and psychological abuse. The stupid thing was, my parents were really intelligent people. Really smart fuckers. They knew how to play the system. They knew how to work everything in their favour. It's a pity that their intelligence was wasted on such fucking horrible human beings.

"I don't ever want to be a person like my parents, if I ever have kids, they'll be loved, cherished…" I sniffled, I'd not told him about losing my baby. That was far too deep a wound to open up again. Richard pulled me against him, his lips softly kissing my shoulders.

"Libby. I'm here for you, always, if you need me, you just call. I'll be there in a heartbeat. Even if I'm on duty. You're someone who I want to be part of my life, even if we are just friends. God knows I want it to be more, but if you're not ready, I can wait."

I turned to face him, my fingers trembled as I reached up and caressed his clean-shaven jawline. "What if I don't want to wait?" I asked, gazing into his eyes.

I smiled at the happiness I saw in their depths. He pulled me down to him, his hands sliding reverently over my body, pulling the long, sleep skirt of the sapphire-blue dress I'd borrowed from Mel up over my hips until I bunched up at my waist.

"Are you sure? I don't want to rush you," he said.

I smiled, laying atop him, I could feel how ready he was. "I'm sure," I said, leaning down to kiss him.

All thoughts of everything else forgotten as we made love in the small room they used for the children's playgroup on Tuesdays, Bible studies on Thursdays, and illicit, powerful, soul-mending lovemaking. Because, you know, what better place to heal our soul through sweet, scintillating sex than on holy ground?

After, I straightened myself up to the best of my ability, Richard lay there, atop the pile of his clothes. I smirked, enjoying his nakedness. I picked up my digital camera and turned it on, taking a few personal snaps.

"Those going in the official photographs?" he asked with a chuckle.

"Maybe not the official ones…" I grinned, leaning back down to kiss him. I moaned softly as his tongue slid over mine. "You'd better get dressed, I have another photo session in about ten minutes." I kissed him again. I got to my feet and saved his sexy pictures to my private folder on my laptop before I deleted them from the digital camera's memory.

I unlocked the door once he was decent and not looking so dishevelled. The room had a little sexy funk to it, but it aired out quickly once I'd left the door open. People started to filter in and out, and Richard stayed by my side, watching the others having their photos taken for the photo books that would be produced and left in the police, fire and ambulance stations.

The evening ended, and Richard helped me to pack up. I sighed as I felt his arms slipping around my middle.

"Come home with me…" he whispered.

I turned, my eyes meeting his. I could see the need, the desire in them. "All right…" I agreed.

We had everything packed in my car in record time, and I followed him back to his place. As soon as his door was open, we were embracing, kissing, fondling, touching… We only made it as far as his couch that first time… Then later the bed, then the shower, then finally back to the bed, where I collapsed atop him in a sweaty, sex-fuelled exhaustion.

The next morning, the sunlight streaming from the open curtains in his bedroom woke me. Richard was already awake and watching me. As soon as I smiled at him, he pulled me into his arms for another round.

As I lay there in a post orgasmic haze, h kissed me once more and got up. I snuck a glance over my shoulder as he stood up, his back to me. He had ink. A beautiful scrollwork with two doves and wedding rings, *'Olivia & Richard always and forever'*, was inked on his right shoulder. I wondered at its meaning, it was obviously some sort of marriage thing… But was it his? He hadn't said anything about being married, and there was no wedding ring, nor wedding band tan on his ring finger.

But still…

What the Fuck?

Chapter Twenty-Three.

Over the next week I spent time working on getting new photos and prints ready for my stall, having lunch with Richard, when we could find the time, spending time with Mel and her new family, and getting more shots of Zane for both our portfolios.

I'd also decided on the fate of the old cottage.

"Okay, so you sure you don't want to fix it up? You can get a lot more for it you know," the estate agent said, as he looked around the front of the property.

"No, list it as a renovator's dream whatever, I just want it gone."

"You have the key? Mind if we take a look inside?" This was the part I wasn't looking forward to.

"Uh… Yeah," I said, fumbling in my pocket for the old key that my lawyers had kept hold of in one of their safety deposit boxes, kept in trust until I was ready to face the old demons that resided there.

If anything about my blossoming relationship with Richard had taught me, it was that in order to grow, I needed to let go. He was there for me when things got dark in my mind, talking to me about things he was doing that day, or taking me to places that I'd been before, but was now seeing through new eyes.

My photography work had changed too. I was taking less photos of dreary places, more light and happy ones, and that was helping the sales at the market stall as well. I had a wedding coming up that was taking place at Mel's family gardens. I was looking forward to it. I loved taking photographs in the gardens. Mel had worked so hard on the place, and it was going to be featured in *English Garden Monthly Magazine*. Quite a prestigious thing for Mel.

But now, I had to face the darkness of the cottage. I pulled the key out of the denim pocket of my jeans and unlocked the door. The hinges creaked noisily, and the dust flew as the air shifted. The estate agent waved his hand as the dust drifted in the shaft of light offered by the open door. He pulled his phone out and activated the small LED light in his torch app, the beam cutting over the abandoned furniture. The scurrying of mice sounded overloud in the house and the smell of animal droppings permeated the air. I ignored it, as memories of my time in hell resurfaced. The estate agent pulled a handkerchief from his pocket and put it over his mouth.

"Upkeep on this place hasn't been kept I see," he noted. Small piles of garbage were still in the corners from when my parents still lived here. There were no pictures on the wall, nothing to indicate this was a happy home, just a place of ghosts and demons.

"It wasn't a priority to me, I never really wanted to set foot in this place ever again." The only response I got was a grunt.

"Well, you'll have to clean it out before we even consider listing it."

I nodded as we left the house. We'd only been able to get in as far as the living area, but that was far enough for me.

"Yeah, I understand." Oh, fuck yeah, I understood, but I wasn't happy about it.

"This could get a good price at auction, if you put a little into it."

"I can't really afford to put a lot of money into fixing the place up. Cleaning it won't be a problem, I can do that. But repairing it? Going to cost me too much." I shook my head. "Look, I just want a quick sale once I've got the place cleaned out."

"All right, once you have this mess sorted, we'll come in and get some pictures and get the auction set up."

"Right." I sighed, wondering how I was going to accomplish this.

I guess I'd need a little help from my friends, and a few days later we began.

I'd called up for a dumpster to be delivered to the cottage, and it was already halfway to being filled and we hadn't even gotten a quarter of the way through the living room. I'd waded through garbage and broken furniture to push open curtains that fell apart in my hands with rot and age just to let in a semblance of light through the grubby windows. I avoided my parent's room until the last. The scent of my father was stale, but still there and sent shivers down my spine. Richard came with me, holding my work-glove covered hand in his as we stepped over the broken remains of my childhood home.

Robbie was going through some old paperwork that we'd found, when he called out to me. I picked my way back through the broken furniture and garbage until I came outside into the bright, cleansing sunlight.

"What's up, Robbie?" I asked, already feeling emotionally wrung out.

"I found your birth certificate, Libby."

"My birth certificate?" I scowled. "Mum said they lost it, years ago," I said shaking my head. Yet more lies I was told.

I reached over and took it, looking over the details… There was one thing that stuck out like a pair of dog's balls.

The name of my father did not match the name of the man who raised me.

I guess I now knew the reason why my 'father' was such an arsehole to me. I wasn't his daughter.

"What the fuck?"

Chapter Twenty-Four.

The sun shone down on the wedding party as the bride made her way to the small altar that had been set up in the Whittaker's gardens.

The bridesmaids wiped their eyes as the bride kissed her father, who had escorted her down the grassy aisle between the neatly-lined seats decorated with white, frilly and fluffy buntings. My camera clicked as I got more shots of the beautiful woman as she approached her bridegroom. The soft murmurs of appreciation came from the congregation of guests as the softly playing harpist finished their piece. Behind the groom, the tinkling of the fountain where Zane had posed for me took over as the natural background music for a beautiful wedding setting.

"Dearly beloved," the vicar began, "we are gathered here today, in the sight of God, to join Gloria and Andrew in holy matrimony…"

I snapped a few more pictures shifting into position in front of the fountain, so I could get a shot of the couple and their guests in the background, not noticing the movement at the end of the grassy aisle as two police officers approached.

"Andrew McKenzie…you are under arrest!"

The shocked gasps of the guests and the shouts of indignation rose as Richard and Lisa approached.

"Shite," the Groom muttered, turning and pushing past the vicar as he bolted… towards me.

I stood in shock as he pushed past me. I lost my balance, toppling into the fountain that was right behind me. The shock of cold water made me drop my beloved digital camera, and unfortunately, my old, trusty SLR was attached to the neck strap, and nestled on my chest as well, ready for use…and not a dunking as it too was currently getting.

I coughed and spluttered as I broke the surface, slogging my way out of the fountain with my poor precious and now ruined cameras in hand. The wedding itself was in shambles. I hauled myself out of the cold fountain and watched as the groom made a break for it, leaping over the small hedge borders, kilt flapping in the wind exposing his very pale arse cheeks with Richard in hot pursuit. The bride wailed, her mascara trailing down her cheeks as she screeched.

"I told him not to do it!"

I sat on the edge of the fountain, letting the water drain from my precious cameras. Hours of hard work gone into the fountain. I shook my head. This could, and probably would ruin me if I couldn't get my cameras replaced. I'd spent pretty much all of my savings on clearing out the fucking cottage, and fixing some of the dire repairs, such as the broken windows and a hole in the roof.

"Fuck," I muttered.

I looked up as a shout from the chase grabbed my attention. Richard had tackled the groom, his kilt flying up unceremoniously over his arse with the impact of runner and earth. There was a small struggle as the groom attempted a futile escape, and Lisa ran to help her partner. Another two police officers arrived to help with the arrest, letting Richard get up and dust himself off. I looked forlornly at my cameras, the digital one wouldn't even turn on, and the SLR had a cracked section in the film compartment casing, which had undoubtedly let light in to ruin the film within.

"You okay?" Richard asked, kneeling down to check on me.

"Bit wet, but I'm okay, my fucking cameras, however..." I sighed. "They're totally and utterly fucked."

"You want to press charges for assault and reckless damages?" he asked.

"You think I'd have a chance at some compensation?"

"You might, but I don't know, depends on the judge."

I sighed heavily. "I won't bother. I can't afford the lawyer fees anyway. Guess I'm about to become an unemployed photographer."

"What makes you say that?" Richard asked, reaching up to push my sopping fringe out from over my eyes.

"These were the only fucking cameras I own." I held them in my hands like dead puppies. "I am ruined." I looked up to see the wailing bride. "And I'm not the only one who's had a shit of a day." I sighed. "You need me to come by and make a statement?"

"I can get it from you now, if you like."

I nodded, letting him lead me away from the bride who began to screech as her groom was led to the police van. I gave Richard my statement. He guided me to the police car and, like the gentleman he was, drove me up to Mel's place where I had my car. Seeing that he was the arresting officer, of course, he had to head back to do paperwork and process the groom.

I walked into the laundry door of Mel's place. Mel, Adam and little Aaron were in Scotland. Adam was wrapping up filming there before he came back for the final shots of the movie being filmed at the Castle.

I pulled off my sopping wet clothes, tossing them into the washing machine and grabbing a towel from the clean laundry basket and wrapping it around myself.

As I headed towards one of the guest rooms to make use of the shower, I heard a strange noise coming from the door. A grunting…squeaking sort of noise. I frowned as I put my hand on the handle and opened the door… To be greeted by another bare arse, and four bare legs…and a kilt on the floor.

Oh fuck…

Uncle Leo was paying a visit to Mrs Del Rosa…

The worst kept secret was shagging on the bed in the guest room I used.

What the Fuck!

Chapter Twenty-Five.

After turning tail and heading to another bathroom to clean and wash my eyes out with bleach, astringent and soap to hopefully erase the image of a naked, humping Scottish arse, I emerged, clean, warm and wrapped in a guest robe. My clothes had been in the wash for a little while, and soon they'd be tumbling around in the dryer. I headed down to Mel's kitchen to make a cup of tea.

A bright, cheery tune was whistled before the bright cheery orange beard of Leon McLeod emerged with a towel wrapped around his waist.

"Morning sunshine." I smirked. "Alison on good form, is she?" I swear the bear of a Scot jumped ten feet high when I spoke. Obviously, he wasn't expecting company.

"Jeezus lass! Give a lad a heart attack won't ye?"

I giggled as he settled down and headed to the refrigerator.

He pulled out a bottle of water, took the cap off and took a long pull of the cold water. "What are ye doin' here Libby me lass? Everything all right? Where are yer clothes?"

"I could ask you the same." I smirked as I sipped my cup of tea.

I swear, his cheeks almost matched the colour of his beard. "Ah, well, I had tae use the shower…"

"Leo, are you coming back…oh!" Mrs Del Rosa's voice drifted through to the kitchen, she'd obviously spotted me sitting at the breakfast bar with a steaming cup of tea.

"Afternoon Mrs Del Rosa." I smiled politely, ignoring the fact that she was wearing a bedsheet wrapped around her body.

"Hello, Libby." She blushed.

"Well, I just need to grab my bag of spare clothes from the room... Then you can have it back," I said, downing my tea and giving them a sly wink. "Don't you two kids do anything I wouldn't do."

I rinsed my cup and left the stunned couple in the kitchen. I dashed up the stairs, ignoring the funk of sex in the guest room as I grabbed my bag and ducked back down the stairs to slip inside the downstairs bathroom and change into dry clothes.

I sighed as I left the beautiful house. Now I had even more reason to sell the fucking cottage. I had to get new cameras. I started my little car and listened to the soothing, pounding bass and drums of *DSS*. Death metal at its fucking finest. I headed back home with my wrecked gear and a heart heavy with worry about what I was going to do.

Back at my flat, I knew the cameras were truly wrecked when I had a better look at them. The Digital still wouldn't turn on, and still dripped water, even now. The SLR was definitely broken too. It rattled when I shook it gently. My cameras were now expensive paperweights.

I fixed myself some dinner and settled in on the sofa, with LP settling on my lap and clawing at my thighs mindlessly, as though they were a pair of pillows for him to plump. I yelped as one of his claws sunk in deep and shoved the pillock off my lap. My eyes went to the coffee table where the damning birth certificate lay. I picked it up and looked at the name of my biological father on the birth certificate.

Lachlan Monroe.

I picked up my laptop and opened up a browser. I typed the name into a search engine and hit enter, results in nanoseconds.

The name hit a few million results, as expected. Most were dead ends, a couple of Facebook profiles of guys who were my age or slightly older, and in no way, could have been my biological father.

There were a few hits though, on recently archived news articles from before I was born, that hit right in the village where my mother had been born. I only knew this, because the place of her birth was listed on the birth certificate. She'd never spoken to me about her own childhood, nor where she'd grown up. And, knowing I'd be in a world of hurt for asking, I never asked. And now, I knew why.

Father Lachlan Monroe had been charged with child sex offences dating back thirty years, and had also been accused of sexual assault of his female parishioners. He was now serving time in prison after having gotten away with it for so many years. I let my mind do the math... It had to be true. There was no other conclusion I could come up with, and it certainly explained why my mother had acted out so much, especially with drugs and getting married to my abusive...whatever the fuck he was to me.

I looked at the picture of the man on my laptop, then pulled my phone out to stare at my own picture, one of me and Mel. We were both smiling in our photograph, the picture of youthful happiness. The image of the man on the laptop was dour, old, he knew he'd done wrong and he knew his time had come to pay for those transgressions against the innocent.

We had the same nose, the same eyes. I had my mother's dark hair and pouty mouth.

My mother had been a victim of sexual assault, rape, which was how I'd come about.

No wonder she hated me.

No wonder she couldn't bear to look into my eyes when she spoke to me.

No fucking wonder she didn't want me.

In all truth, I probably should never have been born.

What. The. Fuck.

Chapter Twenty-Six.

A knock on my front door startled me out of my doom and gloom musings. I set my laptop down on the coffee table, along with my birth certificate. I pushed my skinny arse up off the sofa and headed to the door. Peering through the peephole, I saw Richard on the other side, smiling. My heart warmed at seeing him. I definitely needed to be wrapped up in his arms, to feel loved, like I mattered. I unlocked and opened the door.

"Hey," he said. "You're looking less like a drowned rat now. Glad to see you got home okay." He leaned forward and kissed me softly, keeping his hands behind his back.

I nodded. "Yeah, I am, but my cameras are ruined." I nodded to the drainer on the sink where they were still draining. "They are now some very expensive paperweights."

"Well, maybe these will help." He pulled a gift-wrapped package from behind his back. Wrapped in silver paper with black and purple ribbon, it was obviously two boxes, one smaller one stacked atop a larger one but professionally wrapped.

"Richard, what have you done?" I asked, stepping back into my flat, looking back to him as he followed me.

"Just taking care of my girl." He smiled, settling down on my sofa. "Open it."

I sat beside him, shifting the paperwork from the fucking Cottage out of the way.

I carefully opened the gift wrapped present. I gasped. Sitting amongst the paper were two cameras, two brand-new cameras.

"Fuck! Richard, these would have cost you at least three grand!" I turned to him, shocked that he'd spent that much. "I- I can't fucking accept these!" I shook my head in amazement.

"Yes, you can, and you will," he said, taking the boxes out of my hands. He clasped my hands in his own, bringing them up to his lips, kissed my knuckles. I couldn't help it, I started to fucking cry. "What's wrong?" he asked, concern on his face.

"Other than Mel, no-one else has ever done something like this for me." I sobbed, ugh I hated crying. I'd wasted so many tears over the years on my arsehole parents, but now I was happy. I didn't want to cry because I was happy.

I was pulled awkwardly into his arms, being held was still a little strange, but comforting, and I needed that now. I sniffled as I snuggled into his arms, feeling warm, safe, secure...*loved*.

"I'll pay you back, I promise." I pulled away, wiping my eyes.

"No, you bloody well won't. They are a gift to my girl."

I smirked. "Your girl."

"Yep. Like that huh?"

"Maybe." I ran a hand over the box holding the SLR. I turned to smile seductively at him. "There's something else I might like though…"

"Oh, and what's that?" He smiled. I pulled my legs up underneath me and gently, but insistently pushed on his shoulder, laying him down on my sofa. I gripped the front of his button-up shirt and ripped it open, buttons flying everywhere.

"Hey! I liked that shirt!" he said in mock-distress.

"I'll fix it." I leaned down and kissed his slight six-pack, my hands going to his belt, looking up at him, my eyes caught the decadently sinful lust burning in his eyes. "Besides, you should know, cameras make me kinda horny, especially when I get them as gifts from sexy police officers." I ran my tongue over my lips before I unzipped his pants and slid a hand inside.

He moaned before his hands gripped my hips and he somehow managed to flip us, so I was now underneath him. "Sweetheart, I'll buy you all the cameras in the world if this is what happens!"

His lips crashed against mine, and we made sweet, frantic love on my sofa as Lord Psycho watched, his green eyes widening as we writhed, butt naked on the sofa finding our own fucking Nirvana within each other.

Later, I lay snuggled up on the couch, spooning with Richard while we watched some old television show. His discarded pants started to vibrate. He was asleep behind me, I reached forward and snagged the belt loop of his pants and pulled them towards me. He grunted in his sleep and tightened his arm around my middle. I sighed, dropping the pants to the floor. The impact had jostled his phone out of the pocket and I saw the screen all lit up with the name 'Liv' on it, with a picture of him and another woman snuggled up together and smiling for the selfie before the call rang out and the screen went dark. I leaned back, my face curling into a slight scowl. I wasn't sure exactly who that was, could she be a sister? He hadn't said anything about his family, she could be anyone.

But my mind went back to that fucking tattoo on his back... *'Richard and Olivia, Always and Forever'*

Olivia... *Liv.*

It couldn't be coincidence... Was he married? Was I his side chick? Could my life get *any* more complicated?

What. The. Fuck.?

Chapter Twenty-Seven.

I said nothing to Richard about the phone call. I had to work things out first. He left my flat, after we arranged to go out to dinner the next day. I had nothing else to do, so I called Zane, and we arranged to go out to a local park for another shoot, with my new cameras. I took my time in setting them up while Zane chatted to a gorgeous and obviously gay couple. I took some candid snaps to test out the cameras. They were beautiful, professional quality, and though not quite top-of-the-line, they did a fantastic job.

Over the next couple of hours, I took some fantastic shots of Zane, with high quality pictures on the digital camera, and some excellent shots on the SLR that would make Zane and my portfolios—as Zane put it—'sparkle'.

"So..." he said as we settled into the infamous 'Cock Booth' at Rosie's for a cup of tea, well coffee for him, tea for me. "I have a friend in LA, who wants to help me kick start my modelling career, and she's looking for a new photographer." I set my cup down.

"Really?" I asked.

"Yep. I kinda suggested you, and kinda sent some of your shots to her, and she was excited. She wants to meet you, or at least chat via Skype." Zane grinned. "You know I'm heading back to LA in a few weeks. Can't stay here, this fucking English weather has destroyed my Man Tan."

I laughed, he was starting to look a tad pasty. "What about you and Robbie?" I asked.

"Robbie and I have had fun, sweetie. I'm all for fun, you know that. But we are great friends, with benefits, and

151

that's what we're comfortable with. He knew I wasn't staying here. LA is my home, while this is his."

"You know, I do work, and Richard and I are together, right? If I do accept, then how's that going to work."

"Long distance relationships do work, you just gotta put some effort into it. I mean look at Mel and Adam, he's not home most of the time, but they're always chatting on the phone or Skyping." He stirred his coffee absent-mindedly. "And you did say Danny owes you some vacation time, right?"

Yes, yes, he did, about four months' worth of it… Which would work out perfectly if I took this job and didn't like it. "That's different, they're married. This is all new, we've just started out really."

"Oh? And how many times have you done the horizontal tango with him?" he asked.

"Ahem… A few…." I said, clearing my throat in embarrassment.

"So, it's all fizzle and no bang?" he waggled his eyebrows

"What? No! The sex is pretty damned great, I'll have you know."

"Ew! TMI girl, way TMI!" Zane put his hands over his ears. "I'm gay, remember. Va-jay-jays gross me out, like, totally, blergh!"

"You don't wanna know, then don't ask." I shook my head in amusement while Zane made a show of

152

downing his coffee then reaching for the coffeepot for a refill.

I nursed my teacup.

"So, he bought you those pretty new cameras?" he asked me.

"Yeah there's over three thousand pounds worth of gear there."

"You're getting them insured this time, right?"

"Yes, I most certainly am." Yes, I had been an idiot and not had my old cameras insured, but this time, I'd make sure they were properly covered by insurance, lest I have another camera-tastrophe.

Inside my backpack, my phone rang.

"Hang on a sec," I said, reaching down to my bag. "Ugh, estate agent, I gotta take this."

I hauled myself out of the seat and answered the phone. I stepped out into the street and walked around the side of Rosie's into the small but clean alleyway.

"Hello, Libby speaking," I said as I answered the call.

"Hello Miss Hastings, this is Ernest Young from Young and Bold Real Estate, we just want to arrange the final viewing dates for your property before it goes to auction next weekend?"

Fuck, I'd almost completely forgot about that. "Uh, yes, sure, so this is you guys coming though and then the next day the public viewing, right?"

"That's correct, Miss Hastings, yes."

"And do I have to be there for the viewings?"

"I'd like you to come to the first one, just to make sure you're happy with the process, but the public one, no. You don't need to be present for that."

Inwardly, I sighed, I was glad for that. I didn't want to step foot in that house ever again if I could help it.

Over the last few weeks, we'd finished clearing out the rooms, pulled up the carpets, torn down the old, ratty curtains, cleared the garden of the shed I'd destroyed, and cut the long grass and brambles that had taken over the place. I was surprised at how nice it looked, even without the carpets in it. If I didn't have so many horrible memories associated with the place, and if I had the money, maybe I could have turned it into a nice home for myself…and Richard. Wait…was I really considering long term with him? I sighed, as I ended the call. Maybe I was. Maybe it was time for Libby Hastings —'wild child', to settle down.

In part, I think I was a little jealous of what Mel and Adam had. Happy life, beautiful baby boy, strong marriage and love, lots and lots of fucking love.

Yes, I fucking wanted that. All of it. Maybe, with Richard, I could have it.

I headed back to Rosie's and sat opposite Zane. The look on his face was not good.

"What?"

"Honey, don't panic, but Richard just went across the road to the jewellers."

"Okay, why would I panic?"

"Because, he just walked in there, hand-in-hand with another woman."

"What. The. Fuck?!"

Chapter Twenty-Eight.

I watched, hidden inside Rosie's as Richard walked out with the woman beside him. The pretty lace curtains that covered the lower half of the windows kept us hidden as we peeked over the curtain rail like a pair of naughty children waiting for a glimpse of Santa on Christmas eve, only this time, it was the Grinch.

"Oh, my fucking God," I said softly, watching as they shared a kiss.

My heart broke, shattering into a million pieces as she hugged him and caressed his face lovingly before they walked off, hand-in-hand towards his car, where he, being the fucking gentleman he was, opened the car door for her, then closed it once she was safely inside.

"Breathe honey." Zane had come over to my side of the booth and was rubbing my back as I felt the start of a panic attack settling in. My chest tightened, my vision lured with tears and I trembled in sheer emotional agony.

"Did... I ... Just... Fucking... See that?" I gasped, rocking slightly as I hunched over.

I tried to calm myself. It had been years since I'd had a panic attack, fucking years! The last one was when Danny had shown me the death notice of my 'father'. I don't know why I had panicked then, but all the emotional shit that he'd put me through had raced back through my body, rendering me near insensate with panic. Danny had been there for me then, and I knew he would be there for me again and again, just like Mel, and Zane.

I had a good, tight circle of friends. I could get through this latest shitstorm.

"I had a feeling something was up," I said, finally getting control of my breathing. I sniffled, wiping the tears away.

"Oh?"

"He's got a tattoo, '*Richard and Olivia forever and always*'. Got wedding rings and doves on it, all that lovey shit. There were times when he'd take phone calls and leave the room, and we were asleep on my sofa the other day and his phone rang. I saw who it was. 'Olivia'. There was even a picture of them, all loved up on the screen." I put my hands over my face, trying to stop the stupid flood of fucking tears. "How could I have been so fucking naive? Seriously? Why the fuck can't I find someone who isn't married, like do I have a fucking sign on my forehead that reads *gullible bitch*?" I sighed. "Fuck this, and fuck him. You know what? Call your friend Zane, she if she'll give me a shot."

"OMG! Really?" Zane asked, clapping his hands together so rapidly they were a blur. "Oh girlfriend, you can stay with me! Mel's old room is empty, and I was going to start looking for a roomie bitch as soon as I got back to LA, but squee! This is epic!" he paused, looking at my distraught face. "But honey, you sure you want to do this? I mean, you are in a tizzy right now, and might not be thinking clearly…"

"Oh Zane, everything is fucking clear to me right now. But first, I'm going to go and confirm what my eyes, and you have told me. I'm going to sell that fucking hell hole, then I am so fucking out of here."

"What about Mel?"

I smiled at him. It was sweet he considered our best friend, and how she'd take my leaving the UK for LA. I knew she'd be sad, but she also knew that I had to spread my wings, especially when she heard about this latest fan-fucking-tastic development in my love life—or now, lack of love life.

"Honey, Mel has a whole village to look after her and baby Aaron, Aunty Libs will be back for Christmas, his birthday, her birthday all the rest of those really important milestones."

"And, so will Aunty Zed." He smiled, texting on his phone.

"Uh, no, do not call yourself 'Aunty Zed'. That right there is a *Pulp Fiction* reference that will haunt that baby for eternity. Aunty Zee sounds much better, or fuck even Aunty Zane."

"But it's 'Zed' in the UK, so I'd be literally correct." Zane smirked. I flipped him the bird. But I was secretly glad he'd managed to divert my attention.

His phone pinged with a message.

"Oh! Libby! Laura Rose got back to me! She said you can start as soon as you get here! I said you'll be there in about two weeks!" He squealed like a rabid teenager at some fucking famous boy band concert.

"Well, I guess there's nothing else for it then. Time to give Danny my request for leave. Oh wait, what the fuck am I going to do with LP?"

"See if Mel will take him," Zane said, finishing his text to Laura Rose.

"Hmm, but she's got the baby."

"True… What about Leo?"

"Well…" I smirked, "I do have something that might convince him to take the cat on." I grinned.

"Oooh juicy Goss! Give it up bitch!" Zane demanded. I shook my head. "What and lose my bargaining chip? Not fucking likely." I sighed, pushing up from the bench. "I got a fucking load of stuff to get done now, Zane." I grabbed my backpack, picking my phone up from the table. I noticed there was a message from Richard. "Fucker." I muttered reading it. He'd fucking cancelled our dinner date. I knew why. That was fine, I now intended to pay him a visit this evening, and tell him to fucking sod off.

I sent him a message, alluding that everything was ok, and that I'd see him later.

He had the audacity to send me back a message filled with sappy fucking hearts.

What. The. Fuck.

Chapter Twenty-Nine.

I pulled up in Zane's car, mainly because my little boom-box on wheels would have alerted my prey to my presence. I lifted my hand, fisted to knock on his door and rapped my knuckles against the wooden panels.

"Coming. Just a sec." A female's voice called out form the other side. I heard the words. "Pizza delivery is early." Muttered as they unlocked the door. Pizza, eh? Not quite.

"Hi." I smiled at the woman who had been with Richard earlier this afternoon. "Is Richard here?" she looked slightly uncomfortable.

"Uh, yes, but he's in the shower."

"That's okay, can you give him these for me? Tell him I don't want them anymore, and he can go fuck himself. Though it's obvious, he's fucking you too." I shoved the cameras, boxed back up in their original packaging and turned away from the stunned woman. I heard the door shut, then ten seconds later it opened as I walked down the drive.

"Libby?" His voice cut me like shards of freshly broken glass. "Baby? What's going on?"

I couldn't turn to face him. I kept walking to Zane's car. I felt his hand on my shoulder. "Libby, damnit talk to me!"

He turned me. I was faced with his eyes, confusion blazing in them as he stood naked but for a towel, still dripping wet from the shower.

161

"Fuck you, you fucking, lying piece of shit! Why didn't you tell me you were fucking someone else huh? It's not so bad that I have my entire existence fucked by the fact that my real dad was a fucking child rapist, and that my childhood was so fucked it would fill a psychiatrist's filing cabinet, but oh no, I have to fall for the one guy who gave a shit about me, only to find he's fucking *MARRIED!*" He stopped, looked at me, realisation on his face. "That's right, *CUNTSTABLE DICK*! The registry of Births, Deaths and Marriages has a public records section you know that? Imagine my surprise when I did some research on you tonight, after Zane told me you'd gone into a jewellery shop with your *wife!*" I pushed away from him when he tried to reach for me. "Do you think I'm so fucking stupid? So fucking gullible? What am I? Something to keep your dick wet while you waited for the little fucking wife to move here? Huh? Well, fuck you, I hope you live fucking happily ever fucking after." I pushed him again, causing him to stumble backwards. "You fucking cunt!"

"Libby!" Richard tried to grab me again as I turned, his hand warm on my shoulder, his voice desperate. I pulled back my hand and slapped him as hard as I could, ignoring the stinging ache in my hand at the impact. I'd done something I'd sworn never to do to someone I cared about, I raised my hand to them.

"Just leave me the fuck alone, Richard. We're done." I sobbed. "Go back to your wife."

I spun on my heel and ran to Zane's car, sliding quickly into the driver's seat and pulling away from the kerb so fast the tires squealed.

I was a mess.

162

My life was a mess.

Everything was a complete and utter fucking mess.

I screamed and belted the steering wheel, letting my emotions out as my body trembled with anger, sadness, desolation. I drove, ignoring the blurring in my eyes, being mindful of the speed limits, despite my fractured emotional state. I left the village behind, heading for the one place I knew I could find sanctuary, Mel's.

I pressed the buttons on the keypad, fucking up the code at least twice before I pulled myself together and got it right. The lights were on in the front room as I pulled up, and I knew Mel would be up with Aaron, who was still having a little trouble settling down at night. I pulled up next to her Range Rover, locking Zane's car up before I headed to the front door. Zane was there, standing at the open front door wearing nothing but boxer shorts and an open robe.

"Hey honey," he said, offering me a cup of hot chocolate. "Mel is in the media room with Lil' A-A-Ron."

I giggled through my snotty, teary face. "Oh, I'm sure she loves you calling him that."

Zane smirked, rubbing his shoulder. "Yeah, Good thing we're leaving in a couple of weeks." He reached under my chin and turned my face to the light. "I see you ended it?"

I nodded, feeling my throat tighten again as the tears threatened to break free. I felt my legs weaken and slid down to the front stoop. Zane followed me, sitting next to me and sliding an arm around my shoulders, hugging me against him.

"Has he tried to call you?" Zane asked. I unzipped my backpack and pulled out my phone. He'd been blowing it up with messages and calls, and even now, there was another call coming in. I rejected it, before I turned the phone off. I sighed.

"Honey, it's all going to be fine. We'll get through this, besides, in LA, you might find yourself a nice, sexy movie star, or even a hot rock star."

"Done the rock stars already, though they were death metal, and I was meat in the sandwich," I said with a wink.

"OMG! Who?"

"*DSS*," I said with a smirk, as I wiped yet more fucking tears from my eyes.

"Get the fuck outta town!" Zane playfully slapped me on the arm. "Lars and Jorgen?"

"Yep."

"Ho-lee shit-balls girl! OMG, I would so swap my dick and balls for a Va-Jay-Jay just to get into their pants."

"I thought you said 'Va-Jay-Jays were gross?"

"They are! But I'd go the sixty-four-thousand-dollar question for those two!"

"Who is getting a sex change now, and why are we discussing this on my doorstep where little ears can hear?" Mel's voice drifted over to us from the front door. I turned.

"Hey, Mummy."

I hauled my sorry arse up from the tile steps to hug Mel, being careful of baby Aaron who rested in his swaddle, secure in his mother's arms. I pulled away, looking down at my best friend's baby, he was so adorable.

Zane and I had gone to Mel's after I'd had my near meltdown in Rosie's. Mel had even offered to pay for my flights to LA, which I'd flatly refused. I had enough to get over there, and had put in the paperwork to organise my work visa, with the information that Laura Rose had supplied. The woman was damned efficient. Danny had been sad that I was leaving, but after I explained things, he understood, promising that there'd be a place for me when I got back… *If* I'd told him, if I came back.

"Come on in, you two," Mel said, rocking the baby as he started to fuss again.

I got up from the step, with Zane's helping hand and we headed in to the media room where a movie was on pause. The smell of buttered popcorn and hot chocolate made my stomach growl, and I remembered I'd not eaten since yesterday.

"Here, before the Libby monster breaks free and devours us," Mel said with a smile, as she handed me the bowl of popcorn.

I settled into the large, plush leather recliner and we chatted about LA while the movie played on. After a while, Mel's phone buzzed, she picked it up.

"Hello?" she said, sitting up. I was holding Aaron, who slumbered peacefully in my arms. "She is, and she's safe…" I tensed, knowing who she was talking about. "Well, that's up to her if she wants to speak with you."

She looked at me. I shook my head. "No, she's not interested in speaking with you right now…" Another pause. "Okay, I'll pass on the message, drive safe, Richard." She ended the call. "Wanna talk about it?" Mel asked, looking at me. I shook my head. "Okay, I'm here when you are ready, you know that."

I nodded. I couldn't believe the arsehole had driven all the way out here to try to see me. Seriously, after the scene I'd caused, and the stinging slap I'd given him as a parting shot…

What. The. Fuck?

Chapter Thirty.

For the next week, I hid out at Mel's, only heading out to attend the final viewing of the fucking cottage. I was glad that one tie to my childhood was about to be severed. My plane tickets had been 'gifted' to me by Mel, along with a new Digital SLR camera as a 'going away present'—bitch. And I had gone to my flat in the dead of night, or when I knew that Richard was on duty, to pack up my shit. I'd managed to 'convince' Leo to look after LP while I was away. The big, burly Scotsman took one look at LP and I swear he was in love. So was LP. Fucking traitor cat.

Today was Auction Day. The day that I was going to be free of the shackles of my childhood. Finally, I'd be free of that fucking house where my miserable life started.

I'd turned my phone back on the morning after I crashed out at Mel's place, after I'd ended it with Richard to find so many messages on my phone that the storage was full. I deleted them without reading and then blocked his number. I had to move on. Right now, I was trying to do just that. I waited for the phone call from the estate agents to find out if the place sold. I wasn't expecting a lot of money from the sale, I'd be happy to just get rid of it.

I waited anxiously with Mel while the auction began. I didn't want to have a direct line open to the auctioneer's assistant to hear how the bidding was going. I didn't have a reserve on the place, hoping that that little fact might make it go faster. It would sell for whatever anyone was willing to pay for it, and good riddance.

Little Aaron sat in the baby bouncer, blowing spit bubbles and kicking his chubby little legs around in pure innocent abandon. It made me sad that I'd miss so much of him growing up, but I'd be back in a few months, in time for Mel's birthday.

This time, we wouldn't be having a major pub crawl like we had the last two years. The first time, Mel hooked up with Adam for the final time, ending in where we were now, and last year, the Paps had a field day. After that, Adam had put the foot down, no more pub crawls for Mel. Mel falling pregnant with Little Aaron had put a stop to that anyway. I had a sneaking suspicion that his conception that night was Adams unwitting birthday present to Mel.

My phone rang on the kitchen bench, making both Mel and I jump with fright. Mel tittered nervously, I shook my head and grinned, the sudden ringing had given me a jumpstart to the heart as well. I picked up the phone.

"Hello, Libby speaking."

"Hello Libby, this is Abbigail Asterley, with Klein-Mercer Auctions. I'm please to tell you that your house sold at auction this afternoon, with a sale price of two hundred and forty thousand pounds."

"I'm sorry, what?"

"Two hundred and forty thousand pounds."

"You're fucking kidding me?" I sat back down on the stool, totally stumped.

"I'm certainly not kidding you, there was a bit of a bidding war between a London developer and a local buyer. His name is..." I quickly cut her off, not caring who bought the place, all I cared about that it no longer loomed over my head

"Stop! I don't want to know who bought it, thanks. So, do I need to come in and sign the paperwork right now, or?"

"*Tomorrow will be fine,*" Abbigail said.

"Right, see you then, thanks!" I ended the call, Mel looked at me expectantly.

"How much?" she asked. I was still in shock, I couldn't believe the shitty old cottage went for that much.

"Libby? How much?" Mel prodded again. I was still speechless. Something hit me on the head and dropped to the bench, it was one of Aaron's stuffed toys.

"Libby, for fucks sake, how fucking much did it go for?" Mel's swearing had returned, she'd managed to curb it since Aaron was born, and had even incorporated a swear jar in the kitchen.

"Two pounds Mel."

"What, it went for two pounds?" Mel shook her head, "No way it could have gone for that fucking much."

"Three pounds." I smirked.

"What?" she realised what she'd done. "Fuck."

"Four."

"Shut the fuck up."

"You're up for a fiver now." I grinned. She flipped me the bird.

"Okay, so how much?"

169

I took a deep breath. "Two hundred and forty thousand."

"Fuck me, you are fucking kidding me? That's fan-fucking-tastic! I'm so fucking happy for you."

"That's nine."

"Fuck." I shook my head at her profanity… Though I myself had added to that jar quite a bit. "I had to make it an even ten, besides, I've been a good girl." She grinned, going to her purse and pulling out a tenner. I watched as she reached up above the fridge and slipped the note into the swear jar. "Aaron is going to be so spoilt when this is full." She smiled.

"He's going to be fucking spoilt anyway.

"That's one." Mel grinned. I shook my head and pulled a tenner out of my own pocket, I could afford it, so…

What the fuck.

Chapter Thirty-One.

Over the next couple of weeks, I'd started to get messages from an unknown number, but I knew who it was.

Please, I know you're leaving, don't leave because of ME, we can work things out.

I love you Libby, please, don't end this!

It's not what you thought, please meet with me so I can explain things!

I ignored the messages, I'd heard them all before.

It was D-Day, as in departure day, time to go to LA and the start of my new life. Robbie was driving Zane and me to Heathrow. Mel, baby Aaron and I were snuggled up in the back, Aaron's baby seat taking up most of the room, so it was a little squishy for both Mel and me on either side of him. My phone rang in my pocket, I pulled it out, not looking at the number.

"Hello, Libby speaking."

"Libby, please, please don't hang up the phone." My heart hammered in my chest.

"Why shouldn't I? You broke my heart, Richard."

"I know, I'm so sorry baby, please, where are you? I want to talk."

"About a half hour out of Heathrow." I stared out the window, not really seeing the scenery that passed.

"The airport?"

"Yes, the airport. I'm leaving for LA today. So, goodbye."

"Libby! No, wait!"

I ended the call and sniffled, fucking tears had started to march towards freedom. Mel reached over and put her hand on my arm.

"You okay?" she asked.

"I'm ok." I nodded, my phone started to vibrate with another incoming call, I ended it before it started to ring. I switched it off and pulled the SIM card out. "Well, guess I'll be getting a new number then." I sighed.

"You'll need a new number in the States anyway," Robbie said, as he slowed down to navigate a section of roadworks.

"That's right, and only those who you want to have your number will have it," Zane said, turning in his seat and smiling back at me.

"You'll have fun living with Zane. Just make sure to lock your door, as he likes to wake you up my jumping on your bed of a morning. Oh, and don't let him take you to any movie studios for extras casting!" Mel advised.

"Bitch, turned out fine for you." Zane stuck his tongue out at Mel.

"That's one!" Mel and I both chorused in the back seat. Zane grumbled and fished out a pound and handed it to Mel for the swear jar, as the rule was, when little ears were around, you still had to pay the penalty for swearing.

"In the end, but the middle was hell," Mel admitted as she pocketed the money.

"Yeah, how many times did I tell you NOT to look at the paper, because things weren't as they seemed?" I smirked.

"Too many to count." Mel sighed. She was thoughtful for a moment. "Libby," she looked at me. "Is it possible that you might be taking things out of context with Richard?"

I shook my head. "No, Mel, everything was clear as day. He kissed her in public, on the street for everyone to see. Then, he cancelled our date for that night, so I went to confront him about what I'd seen, she was there, he was in the shower, she answered the door in a robe thinking I was a pizza delivery."

"So, you put two and two together?" Mel asked.

I nodded "Yep. Seems pretty clear to me." Mel sighed. "What?"

"I don't know, it's just, something doesn't add up."

"Yeah, he fucking lied to me."

"That's one!" Zane and Robbie sang from the front.

"Fuck." I muttered.

"Two!" Robbie laughed, checking me in the mirror and holding out two fingers in a peace sign.

"Buttheads," I grumbled, handing Mel two pounds.

"That's…" Zane started

"Not a swear!" I cut him off.

"Cow." He smirked. Oh yes, this was going to be fun.

A short time later, Robbie pulled up in the short-term parking section, and got our bags out while I went and grabbed a luggage trolley to put all our crap on. I had about three large suitcases and two carry-on bags, while Zane had two suitcases and one backpack. Mel had Aaron loaded into his stroller and we headed to the international terminal where our flight was departing from.

We checked in at the front desk and booked our luggage in before we headed over to one of the small cafes to wait until boarding time.

"You'll love LA," Zane said, a wistful look in his eye.

"You miss it, don't you?" I asked, taking a sip of my tea.

"Yeah, but we'll be there soon," Zane said, slurping his coffee.

I finished my tea and nursed Aaron, snuggling with my Godson until the time drew near to head to our gate. We passed through the passenger lounges to a secure section where Mel and Robbie had to leave us. I was teary eyed as I said goodbye to my best friend.

"Oh stop, you'll set me off. You'll see me in two months, my birthday, remember?" she said.

I nodded. "Yeah, I know."

Zane moved in and hugged Mel and then Robbie.

"You take care of each other, okay?" Robbie smiled as he hugged me. I stepped through the security gates.

"LIBBY!"

I turned, hearing my name being called by a familiar voice.

"No," I said softly, shaking my head.

"Come on, sweets, let's get to the gate." Zane put an arm around my shoulders and led me away.

"LIBBY, STOP!" Richard's voice reached me as Zane walked me away.

"Sir! You can't go through there without a ticket!" The voice of the security guards reached me as we moved ever closer to the gate as the boarding call for our flight was announced.

We handed over our tickets and moved to the door just as the shout carried over the noise of the airport

"Libby! She's not my wife!"

What.

The.

Fuck?

Chapter Thirty-Two.

I showed the security guys at the door my company identification card as they searched through my bags. Going through a metal detector was always fun. I had a couple of piercings that seemed to show up, especially the belly button one, and the toe ring on my left pinkie toe. I hopped on one foot and tugged my boot off followed by my sock to show them the toe ring. I was finally let through, after they'd gone through all my bags, and left me to repack everything. I headed to the studio where Laura Rose was working.

Everything was so flashy, it was busy and bustling with activity. I was amazed at how much was going on, from hair and make-up, to wardrobe changed right there in the middle of the floor.

"Seriously, can you not give me one fucking good pose?" The voice of my employer screamed at a hapless model.

I approached her carefully. "Uh, Laura?" I said moving up slowly, so as not to startle the beast

"Who is addressing me improperly?" She turned and gave me such a scathing look that I almost cringed. "I am called Laura Rose, you will call me as such."

"Right, sorry. I'm Libby."

"Ah, yes Hastings. You're late." She sneered. "Right. Those digitals over there need to be uploaded to the computers, then our boys will touch them up. Then I want you to get the next lot of digitals ready for the next model, back up those files in triplicate, one to the laptop, one to the desktop and one to the hard drives under files with today's date and session one. Then format the SD cards, then get me a coffee, skinny Cappu-latte with caramel and stevia, three stevia, not two, not four, but three." She sniffed, and I noticed the tiny crusts of white under her nostril.

Oh great, a fucking coke head. It was obvious the fucking bitch didn't even remember me from our skype conversations. So much for her being super organised. I wondered if Zane knew she was an addict.

"Well. Get fucking on it girl. I'm not paying you to stare at things."

I nodded, so this was me getting experience as a fashion photographer… Back to doing the shit work that some punk kid intern could be doing, instead of learning the finer points of fashion photography from someone who knew what they were fucking doing. I worked through the day, my feet killing me, my head hurting from the constant flashes of the damned camera's studio equipment and my stomach grumbling from the ache of not having any lunch.

And of course, all through the day, Laura Rose ducked into the bathroom for a line of coke when she started to come down. I staggered into the apartment I shared with Zane, exhausted, I collapsed face first on his three-seater sofa.

"Hey Miss Photographer! How are you doing, sweetness?" he asked, leaning against the kitchen doorframe.

"Rough first day?" he asked. I grunted. "You'll be fine, sweetie, you'll get used to it."

I only hoped he was right. I grunted again. "Yeah, it's gotta get better."

The next few weeks went by in a blur of screaming, crying models and orders for stupid caffeine drinks that went cold, and then I was screamed at for letting it go cold. I was screamed at for uploading the pictures to the wrong files, even though I'd done *exactly* as she'd asked me and named the fucking files *exactly* as she'd fucking told me to. By the end of the fourth week, I was a wreck.

I was having trouble sleeping, I'd lost weight from not eating right and I swore I was coming down with a cold.

I was right.

I woke up on the Saturday with a bad cold. I coughed so much that I was sick, and I was barely able to drag my sorry arse out of bed to go pee. My phone rang, the ringtone of one of *DSS's* hits *Kill the bitch* was appropriate for the caller… Fucking Laura Rose.

I answered, my nose all stuffed up and my hearing dulled form the sinus blockages.

"Hello…"

"Where the fuck are you? You know we have a runway shoot today. You'd better get your fucking ass here or you'll be finished in this industry, you hear me? Fucking finished!"

The bitch hung up before I had a chance to tell her I was sick.

"Honey… Are you okay? You look terrible," Zane said as I dragged myself out of bed and into the kitchen for some cold and flu medicine.

179

His Aunt Jessica and her wife Claudia were both visiting. They'd adopted me as their British niece and had kept be entertained with stories of Zane's youth. Jessica worked at a local youth centre, helping homeless kids find a place to stay.

"I'll be okay. Just drug me up with some cold meds and I'll be fine. I have to get to work," I said, even my voice was dulled in my ears, so chocked up with snot and swollen form the infection.

"Libby, honey, you can't go to work like that." Jessica looked at me, concerned.

"I have to Aunty Jess, I'll get the sack otherwise."

"Libby…" Zane started I put a hand up to stop him.

"Zane, I gotta do this," I said, closing the cupboard door and opening another to grab a glass.

I poured some juice and downed the pills, followed by a swallow of juice that felt like I was swallowing razorblades. I showered and dressed, catching a city bus to the fashion show just as the cold shivers of fever racked my body.

Laura Rose was in her element, screeching like a fucking banshee at everyone. Her eyes seemed to glow with wicked glee when she saw me. "This is your last fucking warning, Lucy. Don't think I won't hesitate to have you on a fucking plane back to Australia, and so help me, if you even think of fucking up today, I'll have your job."

I'd had enough. "You know what?" I stood taller, even though my muscles screamed in agony with the cold. "Fuck you, you fucking slapper skank coke-head bitch. I've put up with your fucking shite for weeks. You make people cry, tell them they're fucking no good, when I can see a fuck load more talent in the people you bring down than you have in your fucking little toe." I scowled at the bitch. "Just because you're behind the camera doesn't mean you are the bee's fucking knees, I got more out of working at weddings and debutante balls than your miserable arse. You know what? Take your fucking job and suck it. You were the one who looked at my portfolio and asked Zane to bring me here and work for you, when I could have been living back home where the sun doesn't burn me to a fucking crisp, where I could spend time with my best friends, and try to work shit out with the man that I love…" I stopped, my sickness and anger bringing out the home truth. I began to cough, a harsh, wracking cough that stole my breath and made my stomach cramp.

I turned, leaning up against a table as I felt dizziness take over.

"Fuck…" I mumbled as the room spun around me and I fell to the floor before black spots danced before my eyes before they joined up and darkness took me out for the count.

"Wha… what the fuck…"

Chapter Thirty-Three.

I woke up in the hospital. Zane and his aunt Jessica sat up and watched me worriedly.

"Oh sweetie, are you okay? You gave me such a fright." He reached over and rubbed my hand.

I reached up and touched a sore spot on my head, wincing when I felt the plaster on it, covering a small gash.

"Yeah, head hurts, still feel like shite." Yep, my head was still there, it was fucking pounding.

"No wonder, you took quite a nasty fall, bumped your head on a table on the way down."

"Ahh, I see Ms Hastings is awake." A female doctor entered with a kind smile gracing her lips. "Now, we've run some scans, and you'll be pleased to know your baby is fine."

"Wait... Baby? Doc, what do you mean, 'my baby is fine'...?" I sat up, panic starting to rear its ugly head at the sudden news. "What baby?"

"You weren't aware you were pregnant? You are about six weeks along," the doctor said, moving to my bedside. She took my wrist in her hand, checking my pulse.

"Hmm." She said, looking down at her wristwatch as she checked the seconds hand against my pulse "Your pulse is elevated. I know this is a bit of a shock, but I need you to calm down a little bit for me, okay?" I nodded. Zane looked at me, shock written all over his face. "You haven't been feeling queasy in the mornings?"

"Nope."

"When was your last cycle?"

"About four weeks ago."

"Normal bleed?"

"Eww…" Zane groaned.

"No, very light, actually."

"It's not unusual for a woman to have a small period once she is pregnant. Any previous pregnancies?" She asked me.

I was quiet for a moment, reliving the pain before I answered

"A long time ago." I said softly. Zane's eyes widened a moment.

"Miscarriage, or aborted?"

"Miscarriage," I said softly.

The doctor gave me a sympathetic smile. Zane's eyes went wide for a moment then softened in sympathy.

"I know this is a surprise, but, you're intending to keep the baby?"

"Abso-fucking-lutly," I said, fierce determination in my stuffed-up, nasally voice.

"Okay, so we're going to start you on a course of vitamins that are going to bring your levels up and help your pregnancy, and I want you to start eating correctly."

I nodded. The doctor turned her attention to Zane

"And you, young man, you need to take care of your girlfriend. I take it you're the father?"

"Me? Oh no honey, Libby's my best friend, but she's so not my type. That male nurse from earlier, though, I'd play doctor and nurse with him any day of the week," he said with a wink, the doc chuckled.

"Yes, Ethan is popular with both ladies and gents." She smiled back at me. "Libby, you have a life changing event coming up. Children are the best thing to happen to a woman." She smiled. "You'll be fine, just rest, get over this cold, eat well, reduce stress and in a few months, you'll be welcoming your baby into the world."

I nodded. "Thanks Doc."

"We'll have you out of here tomorrow. Just need to make sure everything is good before you leave. You had a nasty bump to the head."

"Oh, Doc, I'm heading back to the UK in a few months. Is there going to be any problems with me being pregnant and flying?"

"A long as you're healthy, then no, you should be fine to travel." The doctor left us in the ward. I sighed, rubbing the bridge of my nose.

"So, it's Richard's?" Zane asked, already knowing the answer.

"Yep."

"Gonna tell him?"

"I don't know. I guess, I just… Fuck this is complicated," I growled, before I started to cough again.

185

"Easy, don't stress, just relax," Zane said, standing and grabbing the glass of water by my bedside.

"I just… A baby? Shit Zane… I… I wasn't expecting this. I was certain that I was up to date with my shot, what am I going to do? I think I told Laura Rose to shove her job…"

"Actually, she said you told her to suck it." Zane smirked. "She was crying when she called me, said you'd collapsed, and was unconscious, she called the paramedics. You actually made her cry…"

"Bitch made everyone else cry, she had it coming."

"Yeah, I know she was extreme, but she said there was still a job for you. She needs to take some time out and reassess her position. She said she knew she had a problem with her drug use, wants to get help, but couldn't find the way out. I think you gave her the fright, the shove she needed."

"I don't know if I can work for her again, Zane…"

"I understand." Zane smiled. "You rest, we'll talk more later, okay?" he said, turning on the TV above my bed.

We watched some cheesy, crappy soap operas until visiting hours were finished and the horrible hospital food was brought around.

Zane picked me up the next morning when I was discharged. I skyped with Mel as soon as I got home.

"Hey!"

"Hey, Zane said you had an 'incident' yesterday and ended up in the hospital? Hell woman, I knew going to LA was going to be good for you. Is this one of those 'you should have seen the other bitch' kind of incident?"

I chuckled. "Nope, but, I kinda got some news," I said, looking away abashedly and rubbing the back of my neck.

"Ooh, I got some news for you too! But what's yours?"

"Oh, no you tell me yours first." I could tell Mel was keen to tell me.

"Ok, ok, it's big!" She grinned unable to contain herself. "We're pregnant again!"

"Oh, my god! Congratulations! Seriously, if I could reach through that screen and hug the fuck outta you girl I so would do it!"

"Oh, and more to tell you… Your old crappy shithouse cottage? The new owners have done it up, you'd not recognise it, but they have turned it into a bed and breakfast! Richard and Olivia…" she stopped. "Oh, fuck…uh…" I felt my heart clench again. Obviously, he lied to me at the airport when he said she wasn't his wife.

"It's… It's okay," I said smiling sadly. It really fucking wasn't ok, but hey, I can't control things in the world. "So, I guess I know who bought the cottage then."

"Yeah, they redid the gardens with plants form the nursery. Looks nice, I guess," Mel smiled, trying to work out how to save the conversation.

187

"I'm not angry, Mel," I said. "I promise you that, not with you. I just…" I sighed.

"You wish things worked out different, I know." She sighed. "Well, why don't you call him?"

"Can't, I don't have his number, remember?"

"Libby… I have his number." Mel offered

"I… I can't call him, not yet."

"Why not?"

"I don't know how to tell him my baby is his…" My voice was a whisper, but I knew Mel had heard when she blurted out…

"WHAT THE FUCK?"

Chapter Thirty-Four.

Mel looked at me aghast. "What the fuck do you mean 'the baby is his'?" She shook her head in bewilderment "What fucking baby?"

"That's two!" Adam's voice jeered in the background.

"Shut the fuck up, babe, I got a fucking girlfriend emergency, it's called for, completely and utterly fucking called for." Mel turned her head as she shouted back at him.

"I… I guess, when we did the horizontal mambo, we forgot protection…"

"You *forgot* protection?"

I felt shitty enough as it was, though I wanted this baby, this was in a way my second chance at something I'd been denied all those years ago… *Motherhood.*

"Mel…" I said softly, my throat closing up as her barrage continued.

"How could you forget protection! I mean, come on, out of all the guys you've shagged in your life, you never once forgot to get him to cover his knob! How the fuck do you do something like that? How are you going to be able to support yourself and a baby?"

"Mel…" I tried again to get her attention.

"Of the two of us, I mean, come on, Libby… You're a career girl, always have been! What are you going to do? Abort? Adopt? Like seriously, you can't take care of a baby, hell girl, you can barely take care of yourself after a Friday night. How are you going to cope with poop and vomit and screaming, and late fucking nights, especially when the father isn't there?"

It seemed Mel was projecting her unvoiced problems onto me. But still… It made me think.

She was fucking right. *How* did I expect to be able to take care of an eating, screaming poop and vomit machine?

"Well?" Mel asked, seemingly impatient to have an answer right then and there.

"I gotta go…" I said as I ended the connection, the skype logo stared back at me, not as accusing as Mel had been. I put my hands over my face and cried.

Zane came in shortly after, and closed the laptop lid.

"Hey, sweetheart, here, you need this." He smiled softly, handing me a cup of tea. I took a sip.

"Blergh… What the fuck is this?" I said, scrunching my nose up in distaste.

"Decaf."

"Ew… It's toxic, I need my caffeinated tea back…"

"Sorry sweetie, after living with a pregnant Mel for so long, its second nature, nothing but good food and decaf tea and coffee for you now. You've got another life to care about now so you gotta be eating right."

"Great, just fucking great," I groused, but my sneaky hands slid around my middle.

"Just wait until you crave pickles and ice-cream with horseradish and chocolate sauce on top.

"Get the fuck out, that's disgusting!"

"Mel swore by it."

"She never told me that," I mused.

"That one wasn't her finer moments, but she got it. I guess she was embarrassed about that particular selection."

"What, and the sardines with port wine jelly and custard wasn't?"

"Oh my god, if you *ever* pull that one on me… I'll… I'll disown you woman!" Zane made a gagging sound as he walked out of the living room and towards the bathroom. "Fuck, just thinking about that makes me want to puke!"

I laughed my arse off as he slammed the bathroom door and began to retch.

****

I lay back on the sheet covered reclining seat, or whatever the fuck they called it. A tiny little peanut shaped thing was on the screen, blurry, but fucking there. And the heartbeat… Sweet fucking hell, I was in love as soon as I heard it. The ultrasound tech printed off a copy of the ultrasound for me, and circled the peanut-shaped thing that was my baby in a red marker.

I gazed at the image back at the apartment. I was now on the edge of my first trimester. I'd been lucky that my morning sickness was minimal, the same couldn't have been said for poor Mel. She suffered terribly, according to

Zane. I didn't want to speak to her yet, not after our spat. I wasn't ready. But damnit, I knew I was ready for this baby.

I'd been working at Laura Rose's studio, doing photoshoots for her while she was in rehab for her cocaine addiction. I worked differently to how she did. I used the technique's I learned when I was working with nervous brides or debutantes, and the models loved it. Calm music played, giving them a more natural look, which didn't need to be 'photoshopped' as much. The atmosphere was definitely calmer, no shouting, no stress. And the rise in pay was fucking helpful, to say the least. But I wasn't really happy there.

My heart lay elsewhere. It was back home, in the UK.

I looked over at Zane… "I need to go home," I said softly.

Zane smiled. "We're almost there, sweetheart."

I put a hand over the small bump that would undoubtedly grow bigger in the weeks to come.

"No, Zane… I want to go *home*."

Zane smirked. "Took you long enough."

"What the fuck?"

Chapter Thirty-Five.

I shook my head. "You knew all this time, didn't you, that I wanted to go home."

"Well, you kept watching the BBC channels on the cable service, plus you are always looking at the UK newspapers online. And I've spotted you checking out Mel's website for the nursery too many times. You're pining for home, I understand."

"I miss her." I admitted.

"Anyone else?"

"I…" I closed my mouth. I didn't want to admit it, but fuck, yes, I did miss Richard, but I wasn't about to get my heart broken all over again. I'd avoid him. Danny knew some people in London where I could get work as a photographer. Maybe I could even go back to selling my prints, even set up a website to sell them from. After all, I was going to be a single mum soon.

"It's okay, sweets. Mel says she can't wait to see you."

"Really?" I asked, tears pooling in my eyes…

Stupid fucking pregnancy hormones, I fucking cried at the stupidest things… Commercials, puppies, sunsets, homeless bums who stunk of piss and alcohol—those Zane steered me far, far away from. If it was even *remotely* sad, I bawled. I also started to have weird cravings, like Krispy Kreme doughnuts with mustard smothered all over the sugary coating, Ben and Jerry's ice cream—any flavour, partially melted with sardines to dip and devour… I think Zane is forever off any kind of ice cream after he caught me doing that and licking my fingers afterwards.

"Oh my god, it smells like bad porn in here…" he'd groused coming home and catching me sucking melted ice cream and sardine juice of my thumb. "Libby. What the hell are you *eating*?"

"Stuff."

"Stuff that smells like a porno grandma who hasn't showered in weeks." Once he saw what I was eating, he spent the next twenty minutes with his head over the loo while I simply dipped another sardine into the ice creamy, gooey-goodness.

"I got the ultrasound done today," I said, waving the little picture at him when he returned to the living room.

"Can I see?"

"Of course, you can, Aunty Zed." I smirked, patting the sofa beside me after I shifted the empty tins of sardines and the near-empty ice cream bucket. Zane squealed and snuggled up beside me. "There's the head… I think… And there's the arm…"

"Honey, you sure that's an arm? Looks an awful lot like…"

"I won't know the sex for at least another month, that's *if* I want to know," I said snuggling up to him as he slipped an arm around my shoulders.

"I still think that's a weenie…" He smirked, pointing at the spot.

"Arm…"

"Baby's arm holding an apple."

"Wanker…"

"It's a boy, and what a boy!"

"I bet you it's a sweet little girl, and not an icky fucking boy."

"Okay, I'll take that bet." Zane smirked, sticking his hand out.

"What? That it's a boy?"

"Yep, now you tell me what you're going to front for that bet."

"What?"

"Yep, put your money where your mouth is momma."

"Okay… I bet…" I thought for a moment… "Fifty pounds."

"Pfft. Come on, for a big, lifechanging thing like this…. Fifty pounds…"

"Okay smartarse… A big bottle of cognac?" I offered, knowing his penchant for the liquor.

"The good stuff?" His eyes glimmered.

"Like I can fucking afford a three-hundred-pound bottle of that crap. I'm an expectant mother!"

"Oh no, honey, this one is an 1862 cognac. It's like a thousand bucks or more."

"Seriously?" I asked, amazed that someone would pay that much for a bottle of alcohol.

"Absolutely, the *really, really* snobby stuff can go for the price of a new house."

"I'm an expectant fucking mother, you think I'm going to be able to afford a thousand-dollar bottle of booze? Fuck I'll probably need it after giving birth and the first few days of motherhood."

Zane chuckled.

I sighed. "Okay, then if I have to front you some expensive fucking grog, then you have to sort me out with a crib, a changing table and a rocking chair."

"Ooh! You're in the nesting phase already?" Zane squealed with giddy abandon.

I rolled my eyes at him. "No…" I denied, but secretly I was thinking about where I was going to live. I'd given up my flat's lease and my furniture was all in storage, so I'd need to find at least a two-bedroom flat to live in and then I'd have to see if Danny had work for me, like he promised. Fuck, this was going to be hard.

"So, got any idea on where we're going to live when we get back?" he asked.

"We?" I looked at him.

"Yep, 'we'. There's no fucking way I'm going to let you live on your own while 'up the duff'. Anything could happen." Zane put an arm around me, pulling me tight against his side. I sighed, enjoying the warmth of my friend's body.

"Thanks Zane."

"Anything for you, sweetie."

He reached forward and grabbed my laptop, pulling it towards him he flipped the lid open and turned it on. "Now, let's have a look at three-bedroom houses to rent."

He instantly searched for Miltonford properties, there was one that was perfect three-bedroom, two bathrooms and a little conservatory.

"That's perfect." Zane smiled.

"But Zane, that's for sale, not rent."

"I know," Zane replied, sitting back with a smirk.

"And there's already an offer on the house…" I pointed at the little red flag scrolling across the top of the listing."

"I know." He continued to smirk, leaning back against the couch, putting his arms behind his head in a relaxed pose.

"Zane…" I shook my head, trying to figure things out, until it hit me like a bell from above.

"You fucking bought the place?"

"Yep." He grinned at me. "I put in an offer on the place about two days ago. They need to update the website. The offer was accepted this morning. We own a house!"

"But…but… How can you afford that?"

"While we were back in merry old England, my father passed away," Zane said, his eyes showed a touch of sadness.

"Oh, I'm so sorry." I reached over and wrapped my arms around him in a consoling hug.

"It's okay. He was a rich old bastard who didn't approve of my 'lifestyle choice'," he said, putting the last two words in finger quotes.

"Oh."

"Yeah, basically told me to get my 'faggoty ass out of his sight and never darken his doorstep again'. When I came out at sixteen. I was homeless for about two weeks before my aunt Jessie found me and took me in. She and her girlfriend were very understanding of my situation, having gone through the same with my grandparents." Zane sighed, putting an arm around my shoulders.

"My aunts looked after me until I was eighteen, then I left and moved out to LA, away from all those bigoted fuckers back home. My aunt told me he'd died while I was over at Mel's place, just before Aaron was born. She'd said that no-one was named in his will, so she took some papers to court to claim the inheritance on my behalf, saying she was his only living relative, and then deposited the old man's money into my bank. So, you can imagine my surprise when she sent me a message, saying there's something in there from my father's estate, and it was pretty much all of his money."

"How much?" I asked, then realised how rude that sounded. "Oh, never mind, forget I asked."

"Three-point-four million," Zane said, as if it were nothing.

"Three-point-four million dollars?" Holy shit... I was snuggled up to a gay millionaire.

Who had just bought us a house in England.

What. The. Fuck!

Chapter Thirty-Six.

I looked at myself in the mirror, rubbing my hands over my swelling belly.

Yep, there was a definite bump there, and it was growing.

I was now at my twenty-fourth week. I'd been away from home for almost five months now, and I was feeling homesick. Though we had planned on going to the UK two weeks ago, Zane's Aunt Jessica had discovered she had stage three breast cancer, which had sadly progressed to stage four. After they'd found the first lumps, it had spread through her body at a rapid rate.

Zane had spent many hours at her bedside as the fucking disease took another good woman down. His aunt's wife sat on the other side, softly weeping as her beloved slowly succumbed to the pain.

I kept vigil with them when they both were too exhausted, both emotionally and physically, letting them go and rest, or shower or eat.

"Libby," Jessica called to me as I sat reading a pregnancy magazine while Zane and Claudia, Jessica's wife both went and refreshed themselves.

"Yes, Jess?" I leaned forward, reaching out and taking her frail, pallid hand.

"I want to ask a favour of you."

"Anything."

"I want you to take some photos of us, of me and Claudie, and Zane. Can you? I don't want them to remember me in this horrible state."

"Of course," I said, my mind quickly going over everything I'd need. "When do you want to do this?"

"Soon, but not here. I don't want to die here." She sighed. "One of the orderlies here, he helps terminals like me pass easily. I have the drug that will ease me out of this pain and let me die with some dignity." She sighed softly. "But I don't want to let Zane or Claudie see me suffer. I want to go out on my own terms, happy, free, loved. I want a good day. Can you help with that?"

I nodded, feeling the tears prickle against my eyes as I closed them. "I can, and it would be a pleasure and an honour to help you."

"Good. Thank you." Jess lifted my hand to her lips and kissed the back, before she pressed it against the dry skin of her cheek. "Can you organise a few things for me? There's a park where Claudie and I got married, I'd like to be there when it is time. I'll convince her to take me out of this hole for a day, get the paperwork done."

"You know, this can implicate me in your death," I said, whispering the words.

"You didn't know a fucking thing about this." She smirked. "I only asked you to give me a good day and be my photographer, so my loved ones can have some good memories before I die."

I nodded. "Okay, one good day coming up." I smiled.

"Hey, you two. What are you up to?" Zane asked, coming in with a decaf tea for me and a strong cappuccino for himself.

"Nothing. Aunty Jess was just telling me what a shit you were in your teens," I said, reaching for the decaf, though it wasn't normal tea, it was still hot and sweet, and almost perfect.

Jess laughed. "Wasn't he just." She smiled at the memory. "I want to tell you how much I love you, Zane. If I had been able to have kids, I'd have wanted them to be as wonderful as you. It doesn't matter how you were raised, Zane, it's how you became the person you are today. A good, generous and loving young man, who deserves more than he got in life."

Claudia entered, her hair was still damp from her shower, and wearing clean clothes.

"Right, now we're all here," Jess said. "I want to get the fuck out of here. I want us to have a nice day together. Libby is going to help with her photography skills. Zane I want a nice picnic lunch, Champagne, oysters, the works! And Claudie, I just want you there with me." She gazed lovingly at her wife who looked ready to burst into tears.

"When did you want to do this?" Zane asked.

"In a couple of days, then, we can all rest." She smiled softly.

****

The next couple of days went by in a blur, the knowledge that Jess was going to leave this world by her own hand this afternoon bore down on me, but I had seen the pain in her face, the darkened circles of exhaustion and pain under her eyes. I'd seen the weakness sapping her strength as the horrible disease that is cancer took days, weeks, months and years from her life.

Now, at her choice, she had only hours.

The sun was bright, the day beautiful, warm but not too warm. One of the make-up artists I knew from my job working for Laura Rose had come over and managed to give Aunt Jess some colour to her face. Her eyes were even brighter than normal. She revelled in the warmth of the sunlight, breathing in the sweet, fresh air.

Just getting out of the hospital had been an effort. At first the staff were dead set against it, until she managed to convince her doctor that it wouldn't do her any more harm than what the cancer was doing already, and that she needed one good day before it all went to shit. Her doctor agreed, and we were allowed out of the hospital. Aunt Jess changed into a nice pants suit, and the IV of pain medicine hanging from a stand attached to her wheelchair as we left the sterile and impersonal hospital environment.

Three flute glasses of champagne and one of orange juice (for me) were clinked, and toasts were made as we sat underneath the tree where Jess and Claudia had taken their vows five years ago. Jess slipped the drug into her glass. Though we all saw it, we would deny it.

"It's time," she said softly.

"Time? What was that you put in your glass, Jess?" Claudia asked.

"You know what it is, baby. It's my last hurrah." Jess smiled, she downed the champagne. "I've got about five to ten minutes left. Now, come, let me hold you until I go."

Claudia's eyes brimmed with tears, she let out a sob before she slipped in behind her wife's back and held her, speaking softly. Zane and I kissed her on the cheek, our final goodbyes, before we stood, and left the two women alone in Jess's final moments.

I watched as Claudia hugged the stull body of her beloved wife, sobbing, heartbroken.

"I wonder if I'll ever have a love like that?" Zane asked the cosmos.

"She told me she was going to do this," I said, feeling my own tears break free. "Maybe I should have told her no, but, you know, she was ready."

"What the Fuck?"

Chapter Thirty-Seven

Zane looked at me, aghast. "She told you she was going to do this? Why didn't she tell me?"

"I don't know, Zane," I said, packing away my cameras. "Maybe she didn't want to stress you out."

"But you're pregnant, Libby. The stress of this knowledge, not to mention any repercussions of this, you could go do jail."

I held up a hand, stopping him. "Stop. She wanted this. She did this because she was suffering, Zane. Watching you and Claudie enduring her death was killing her emotionally, she didn't want that."

I turned and looked at the couple, one holding the other, who lay as still as a stone. I knew the drug had done its work.

"Go to your Aunt Claudie, she needs you, Zane," I said, placing a hand on his shoulder. He nodded, pulling me in for a hug before he turned to comfort his desolate aunt.

****

The funeral was a week later. Zane held up well, and there was nothing said about her death away from the hospital. Apparently, it was done quite a bit by other terminally ill patients who were nearing their end. A final, good day with their loved ones, then a sip from a poisoned cup, and oblivion. Unconsciously, I kept my hands protectively over my baby bump, though protecting my unborn baby from whom, I still didn't know.

We left for the UK a week later, finally setting foot on the plane, Zane getting us first class tickets. I felt nauseous on the flight over, plus I had to pee, like, every half an hour. Added to that, I couldn't take a crap, and, to make things worse down that end of the world, I had fucking haemorrhoids! It hurt to fart, and I didn't trust a burp. Heartburn was kicking my arse.

I was miserable.

Until I felt that first flutter.

"Oh my god…" I said, sitting up, putting a hand to my big belly.

"What?" Zane jerked awake, spilling his packet of nuts everywhere.

"I felt something."

"What? A contraction? You're too early!" Zane began to panic, reaching up and pressing the call button for the stewardess to attend his seat.

"No, you tosser." I smiled. "The baby kicked." I grabbed his hand and placed it over my bump. "Wait hang on…" the flutter came again, stronger

"There!" I smiled. Zane had a curious look on his face.

"Fucking. Wow." He smiled, his eyes as wide as saucers.

"Is everything all right?" The stewardess asked as she stopped by Zane's seat.

"Oh, yeah, sorry, false alarm," Zane said sheepishly

"Baby's kicking, and he thought I was having contractions." I smiled, shaking my head.

The stewardess nodded. "No, problem, would you like some more nuts?" She indicated to the scattered remains of Zane's snack.

"Oh, yeah, uh, sorry." He leaned down to scoop the scattered snacks back into their packet, before handing them to the stewardess.

"No problem." She left.

"Oops," Zane chuckled.

"Arse." I snorted, before I settled down and tried to sleep. The baby kicked again, right in my bladder. "FUCK!" I got to my feet. "Move, now, out the fucking way, pregnant lady, gotta pee!"

"But you just peed, like ten minutes ago." Zane got out of his seat to let me and my belly past.

"Yeah, I did, but the little bastard just kicked me, and now I gotta pee again!" I stumbled slightly, as the plane hit some slight turbulence.

The seat-belt sign dinged.

"*Ladies and Gentlemen, this is Captain Franks. We're heading into some inclement weather, and the seatbelt sign has been turned on. We'd like you to please, fasten your seatbelts, as this could get a little rocky. Nothing to worry about, it's a very mild storm but we are expecting some turbulence.*"

"Oh, great," I grumbled as I held a hand under my belly to try to pull up some of the weight from my bladder.

"Miss, you'll need to return to your seat," a stewardess said, stopping me from moving forward.

209

"I need to use the lavatory," I said, trying to move forward.

The stewardess put a hand up. "I'm sorry miss, but you have to return to your seat."

I saw red. "Look lady, I am twenty-six weeks pregnant, I'm peeing like a racehorse every half hour, and right now, the baby just kicked me square in the fucking bladder. If I don't get to the lavatory right now, there's going to be a mess, and I'm not sodding cleaning it up."

The stewardess sighed. "Fine, but the first-class lavatory is out of order. Someone clogged it up, so you'll have to use one in the economy section. It's down the back of the plane."

"The back?"

"Right up the back."

"Shite," I muttered as I waddled down the aisle towards the curtained section that separated first class from the unwashed masses.

Children cried with ear-piercing wails and men who were almost as fat as I was, were squished against poor little old ladies. I groaned as I waddled through, my body screaming out for release as I held tight. The door to the lavatory in the back was in sight. But so was the 'engaged' sign.

"Nooo!" I moaned as I waddled up to the lavatory door. I knocked as politely as I could.

"Someone's in here!" A man's voice called.

"Yeah, fuck off!" A woman's voice joined in followed by moans and rhythmic thumping against the door. The fuckers were joining the Mile-High Club just as I was trying not to piss my fucking pants

"You've got to be fucking kidding me." I whimpered as I crossed my legs as a bit of turbulence jostled the plane. "Hurry the fuck up, pregnant lady, gotta pee!" I banged my fist on the door.

The banging got harder, the moans louder. My urge to pee became uncontrollable as the baby kicked again, hitting my bladder.

"Oh... Oh no..." I moaned as I felt my body give in and the sweeping warm wetness covered my crotch and thighs. "No, no, no, no, no, no!" I cried softly at the state of my light-coloured pants, which now had a dark, damp patch in the crotch.

"Yes, yes, yes, OH GOD EDDIE! YES!" Came the scream of rapture from the lavatory as the thumping finally finished.

The door opened a moment later and a dishevelled redhead and a portly bald man in a cheap business suit ambled out. "All yours doll." He winked.

"Fuckers," I grumbled, heading in to the lavatory to try to clean myself up. I closed the door only to find they'd left a 'present' in the sink. Their used condom.

"What the Fuck..."

Chapter Thirty-Eight.

Thankfully, the stewardesses were helpful, and Zane was able to grab a spare pair of pants and underwear from my carry-on. I sobbed at my misfortune in the privacy of the lavatory, holding myself up against the wall to counteract the turbulence. Of course, little mini-me decided to settle down after my lavatory fiasco and I rested uncomfortably for the rest of the flight while Zane slept soundly.

We landed at Heathrow a little bit delayed by the storm, which was worse than the pilot had told us. We'd had to fly around it, all the way down to Wales before we were able to get a path into Heathrow.

I was exhausted, having barely slept or eaten on the flight.

I noticed the pudgy asshole who had joined the Mile-High club kissing and embracing a woman with three sweet little girls. I stalked over to him.

"You've got a lot of fucking nerve, shagging some redhead slapper in the lavatory while your wife and daughters are waiting for you," I said with a snarl.

"What? Eddie? What's she talking about surely you've not gone back to her again?"

"Oh, again. Eh, Eddie?" I turned to the wife. "Sweetheart, once a cheater, always a sodding cheater."

I turned away from the man who was now redder than one of Mel's roses with embarrassment, and the haranguing he was getting from his good wife.

Zane had watched from the luggage carousel, collecting our bags. He laughed as I returned to his side.

"Libby, that was the fucking best!" he snorted with laughter, piling our bags onto the trolley.

We passed through Immigration, the customs officers stamping our passports. A joyous shout erupted as we passed through the doors to British soil.

I looked up to see Mel, Robbie, Adam, who held little-but-not-so-little Aaron, and Mel's parents. Robbie and his mum held a "Welcome Home Libby and Zane" banner. I smiled.

"Oh wow. This is f—," I stopped, remembering I'd have to pay up if I dropped the F-bomb, "flipping amazing!" I smiled.

Mel rushed forward, her belly slightly bigger than mine. We bumped bellies like a pair of idiots wearing those ridiculous inflatable sumo wrestler suits.

"Oh, my god, look at you!" Mel gushed.

"Look at me? Nuh-uh Mel! Look at *you!*" I smiled.

"Oh, you've seen me like this. So tell me, twenty-five? Twenty-six?" She pulled back from my preggers-hug attempt and looked down at the swollen belly that I sported.

"Six, almost seven." I sighed. "It gets easier, right? Please, tell me it gets easier?"

Mel laughed. "You were there the last time, remember?"

"Uh, yeah kinda." There were some things I was struggling with remembering, like where I put the car keys, and appointments that I'd made but forgot about until my phone reminded me.

"Got baby pics?" Mel asked.

"I do." I reached into my purse and pulled out a few copies of the few ultrasounds I'd had.

"Oh my gosh!" she pointed to the questionable limb "is that a...?"

"La-la-la-la-la-la I can't hear you, no it's not a weenie la-la-la-la-la!" I sang, putting my hands over my ears.

Zane laughed. "We have a bet going on, if it's a boy, I get a three-hundred-pound bottle of cognac, if it's a girl, I get her baby furniture."

"Well, we will just have to wait and see who wins then," Adam said, bouncing Aaron in his arms.

"It's a boy." Mel smirked.

"Oh fu-*fudge*, not you too!"

"I'm having another boy." Mel grinned.

"My sympathies," I said without any real sympathy.

Mel looked at the ultrasound. "Can I keep this one?" she asked.

"Sure, I have a couple of copies spare."

"I did that too, made copies."

"I know, you gave them out as cards for your baby shower, remember?"

"That reminds me! We are having a double shower, you and me!"

"What? A double baby shower?"

"That's what I said!" Mel smiled, as she linked her arm in mine and we waddled through the airport.

"When?"

"In two weeks, then the week after, we celebrate me getting another year older!" Mel cheered.

"Bloody hell, you're in good spirits."

"I got my best friend back home where she belongs!" Mel grinned, pulling me in for an awkward hug. I felt the familiar fullness in my bladder that heralded even more doom for my pants if the loos were all occupied again

"Ugh, I gotta pee, and I'm dying for a shower."

"Yeah, we don't want another accident like you had on the plane. I don't think we have any more pants that are in easy reach." Zane smirked.

"Why? What happened on the plane?" Mel asked.

"Zane…" I warned.

"She peed herself, while a couple were joining the Mile-High club in the only working bathroom on the plane."

I felt my jaw drop. "Zane!"

Oh, my fucking god, I was mortified. Seriously?

What. The. Fuck?!

Chapter Thirty-Nine.

Zane, Robbie and Adam had left us girls to prepare for our double baby shower. Mel's mother had fluffed and fussed around us while we drank mocktails and 'helped' by bitching about our pregnant bodies.

"Oh my god, I need to burp and fart, but I'm too scared to," Mel said.

"Why?" I asked, resting my feet on the ottoman. My ankles were swollen and my back ached, and perched under my arse was one of those doughnut pillows to rest my weary haemorrhoids.

"I'm scared I'll shit myself."

I snorted my mocktail and ended up laughing and coughing so hard that I almost peed myself—almost.

"Well, that was a little too close for comfort. I'm heading to the loo."

"Not if I get there first, bitch," Mel said, hauling herself up with a grunt.

"Like hell woman. I'm not as fat as you. I got speed on my side!" I hauled my own pregnant body up out of the chair, the pillow under my ass sliding to the floor at my feet.

Mel and I waddled with as much speed as we could awkwardly muster towards the nearest bathroom. Though there were plenty in the house, Mel's place being a fucking mansion and all, it was still the thrill of the race and the taste of victory that spurred us on in our childish dash to the toilet.

"Don't be too long girls, our guests will be here any minute!" Mrs Whittaker called.

"Yes Mum!" Mel shouted behind me.

I squealed and giggled as I tottered on my swollen ankles towards my goal, the silver-trimmed handle of one of the downstairs bathrooms.

"I win!" I shouted, as I turned the door handle and flung myself inside.

"Cow!" Mel teased banging on the door good naturedly before she shuffled off to the next nearest loo.

I spent a little more time than I anticipated in the bathroom, nature's callings and all that. I finished up and headed back to the living room where the party was starting. There were several unfamiliar faces there, though one that was vaguely familiar, but I wasn't sure where I'd seen her. I settled back down on my seat, Mrs Whittaker had placed the doughnut pillow back in its place for me before I eased myself back down.

I nodded and smiled to those women I knew, and smiled in what I hoped was a friendly manner to those few I didn't. Mel squealed and hugged the strangely familiar woman.

"I'm so glad you could make it, thanks for coming."

"I wouldn't miss it, after all, you've done so much to help us these past few months."

"Well, we're all here. Excellent!" Mrs Whittaker smiled as she came in with a box.

"What's that, Mum?"

"Oh, it's a cake that Alexandra dropped off for you. She said she was sorry, but she had to deliver a birthday cake to a ten-year old's party, else she'd have been able to stay."

"Well, I'm sure she outdid herself, like she usually does." Mel smiled, while Mrs Whittaker put the cake down on the coffee able. "We'll dig into that soon girls, first, let's play some games!"

"Okay so first game up is called: 'My Water Broke!'" Mrs Whittaker smirked, holding up a tray of cups. "We have these cute little plastic babies in ice cubes, these represent the time it takes for a baby to come along, now, we each take a cup, and the first one that melts wins!" She began to hand out the cups. "We have some beautiful chocolates as prizes. This one takes a while, so we'll get to our next game: 'Baby Price is Right!'"

We watched as Mrs Whittaker pulled away a tea-towel that covered a bunch of baby items, along with hand-written price tags that were lined up neatly in front of the items.

"Now, we need to guess which item cost what! Who wants to go first?"

After a few rousing rounds, Mel's mother began the next game, though it was a little icky, it was still ridiculously fun, 'Test the nappy.' We each had five nappies, and each had a gooey-brown mess within. We had to taste the contents of each nappy and identify what it was.

"Chocolate Pudding!"

"Milky Way!"

"Marmite!"

"Gravy—or I hope it is!"

"Choc-hazelnut spread!"

"What the hell are you crazy women doing?" Zane's voice carried over the laughter.

His face was priceless, he gazed at the crazy women in the room, each of us holding a nappy, some had brown gooey stuff on their face, Mel had chocolate pudding on her nose and a huge grin on her face. I licked the gravy from my lips.

"Well, how else do you expect us to figure out what the baby's been eating?" I asked, standing up with a huff. "Here, try it, tell me what you think." I grinned, offering up the nappy to Zane.

"You all are just crazy." He shook his head.

"Anyway, Adam said there was cake?" Zane reached for the box and flipped open the lid. His girlish scream echoed down the halls of Mel's mansion, had Aaron not been sleeping, he would have been woken by 'Aunty' Zee's girlish wail.

"OH MY GOD! WHAT THE FUCK IS THAT?" Zane was posed dramatically, his hands on his cheeks in shock, his eyes and mouth wide. "That's—oh my god, so disgusting. Even worse than the poopy diapers you were licking! I can't believe you're going to *eat* that!"

He retched and ran towards the bathroom I had raced Mel for not two hours before. Every woman got up and peered into the box.

The cake was an imitation of a woman giving birth. Showing the most intimate parts with a doll's head poking out. The uproarious laughter filled the room as Mel and I both hefted the cake out of the box and together we cut it, taking the doll's head off first, before we cut into the delicious cake beneath.

We all took a piece and settled out in the garden, enjoying the late afternoon sunshine.

The strange woman approached me. "Hello, you must be Libby? I've heard so much about you." She smiled, offering her hand. "I hear you're a wonderful photographer. I was wondering if you'd do some work for me?

I quickly dabbed the crumbs from the cake off my lips with a paper napkin and took the woman's offered hand. "Yes, that's me. Sorry, I didn't catch your name?"

"Oh, Olivia, Olivia Handcock."

Olivia fucking Handcock

Richar- *Cunstable* Dick's *wife* was here, was talking to me. Did she know? Did *He* know? Were they going to try to claim custody of my baby? My heart rate went up a few thousand beats per minute.

"Nice to meet you. If you'll excuse me, I'm not feeling too well." I was suddenly feeling pretty fucking poorly.

What the fuck was she doing here? I headed back inside and glanced back once I was in the shadows of the kitchen. She and Mel were chatting like old chums, even hugging and smiling,

Mel... The woman who was supposed to be my best friend was hugging the woman who was married to the man who had ripped my heart out.

What. The. Fuck?

Chapter Forty.

I hid in my room for the rest of the day while the party wound down. My hands swelled up and I was so hot that I lay in my underwear on top of the bed with the overhead fan whirring away silently above me. I felt dizzy and nauseous and generally crap.

I'd drawn the curtains to shut out the world and its betrayers, and curled up in what was my best guess at a foetal position, my legs and arms protecting my baby from the woes of the world.

"Don't you worry, baby, Mumma's here. Mumma's going to make sure you are loved and cherished."

Unlike my own childhood, I was going to give this kid everything they'd need to be happy and healthy.

A few hours later, Zane knocked on the door. I'd been sleeping, trying to get rid of a headache that was verging on becoming a nasty migraine.

He flipped the light switch on and looked at me. I winced covering my eyes with my arm.

"Bugger off, Zane."

"Nope. Mel was worried about you, Okay? Apart from that gross ass cake, everything at the baby shower was fine, what gives sweetheart? Are you getting bitchy this far in your pregnancy?" he asked me before moving to my bedside.

"I'm really not feeling well, Zane," I muttered, another round of vertigo hitting me. I moaned. "Oh god, get the bucket."

I felt my stomach churn as Zane ran and grabbed the bin from the en suite bathroom, holding it under my chin as I puked up the cake and everything else I'd eaten.

"I thought your morning sickness was over?" Zane asked. "Honey, are you coming down with something? Your face is swollen a bit."

"Dizzy…" I moaned, clutching the edge of the bin as I heaved again.

"Stay right there, I'm going to get Mel." he said, leaving me in my misery.

Mel came soon after, followed by Adam who was holding Aaron.

Everything was blurry, and I just wanted everyone to stop talking so loud.

"Shh, not so loud, I have a splitting headache," I moaned.

"Honey, we're not talking loud at all. I think we need to get you to the doctor, you might have preeclampsia," Mel said, pressing a cool cloth to my head. She turned to Adam. "Baby, can you call ahead and see if Doctor Forrest is on tonight?"

I barely noticed Adam nod before Mel was bustling around my room, gathering a nightgown and a robe and getting Zane to help me get dressed. I felt floppy and dizzy and everything was just blergh.

Adam and Zane carried me 'chair style' to the jeep, while Mel called her mother to come and care for Aaron while they took me to the hospital. Zane sat beside me in the car, an ice cream bucket at the ready in case I was sick again.

The hospital admitted me after running a few tests, and the doctor determined that I indeed had preeclampsia. The next two days were a battery of tests and ultrasounds to ensure the baby was okay.

"Pee into this cup."

"Let's take your blood pressure,"

"How are you feeling today? Any changes?"

"This gel will be cold."

"Here, take these, they'll lower your blood pressure."

I was so sick of hospitals, but at least I was able to pee on command, thanks to the melon sitting in my belly. Finally, I was being released back into the wild, with orders for bed rest and to take things easy until the baby was born

Zane was wheeling me out of the hospital entry in the required wheelchair when an ambulance came screaming up to the emergency entrance. A police car came screaming in to the car park, parking in the police parking space and none other than *Cuntstable Dick* got out. He didn't even spare me a glance as he raced inside, following the paramedics and the unfortunate person on the gurney.

"Get me home, please Zane," I murmured.

"Okay sweetheart."

"Hey, how long until we get the new place?" I asked him.

"Not long now, another month then we can move in."

"Good, I can't wait. I don't like being underfoot at Mel's place," I admitted.

"Oh honey, she loves having you there, you know that. Besides she's missed you."

I grunted, it certainly didn't fucking seem like it the way she was hugging and laughing with Olivia fucking Handcock.

I was quiet on the drive back to Mel's and we came into the kitchen to a sombre mood.

"What?"

"Lisa was injured and has been flown to London," Mel said, sitting at the table with a cup of tea.

"How?" I asked, settling down with a grunt in the seat next to her.

"Apparently, she and Richard had stopped a drunk driver. He tried to get away and he ran her over."

"Oh my god," I said, feeling horrible for the poor woman. "That must have been them at the hospital," I said, looking to Zane.

"We're going to send her some flowers and a card, though there's not much we can do right now, just wish, pray and hope for the best," Adam said, rubbing his wife's shoulders. He turned his attention to me. "You need to go rest, I've set up some movies in the media room for you, there's popcorn and chocolate, Mel, you should go join her."

Mel nodded and we both stood up. I took my best friend's hand and we waddled to the media room, where the title screen of a movie was waiting on the rear wall, the light from the roof-mounted projector shining in the darkness.

"She'll be okay." I said to Mel.

"Yeah, I hope so, she's such a wonderful person, gives her all to the community. So is Richard," she said trying to steer the conversation away from the morbid subject.

"Mel, don't."

"You need to tell him, if you don't." She paused.

"If I don't tell him then what? You'll tell him?"

"No, Olivia will."

"What the fuck?"

Chapter Forty-One.

"She knows, Libby. She even saw the ultrasound."

"Where the fuck did she get the ultrasound?" I asked, feeling my blood boil.

"From me," Mel admitted.

"Mel…" I stood up, the movie forgotten. "You fucking didn't."

"I did, Libby. He deserves to know. It's for your own good. You know this. You'll regret it otherwise."

"Yes, he does, and I'll tell him soon," I said.

"But when? When you're pushing that kid out? When it's his first birthday? When he asks who his daddy is?"

"When I'm good and fucking ready!" I shouted.

I turned and stormed out of the media room and up to my guest room I packed my shit and made some calls to a local motel. I wasn't going to fucking stay here any longer.

"Libby, what are you doing?" Zane asked.

"I'm fucking leaving. I've had it with everyone here. Everything they do, they say, or believe is for my own good. You know what? My fucking parents said that every time they beat me, every time my weak cunt of a father put his joint out on my arm. I know when I'm not welcome, Zane." I zipped up my bags and hauled them from the bed, feeling a slight twinge in my back. "Fuck," I moaned.

"Libby, stop right now, you'll hurt the baby," Zane said sternly.

I stopped and looked at him. In my anger, I hadn't even considered the little one growing inside me.

"Oh fuck." I sat down heavily on the bed, the bag forgotten at my feet. "I'm a terrible mother." I burst into tears.

"Libby, no, you're not a terrible mother." Zane sat beside me, his arms going around my heaving shoulder as I sobbed. "You're going to be a kickass mom who loves her kid to bits."

"What if I tell him, and he doesn't want to be a part of the baby's life?" I sobbed, my words broken between trying to breathe through my snotty nose and the tears that cascaded down my cheeks.

"Then that's his choice. You can't say you didn't try, unless you don't try at all." He hugged me tighter. "Listen, we have Mel's party coming up next week. He's going to be there, why don't you tell him then?" I nodded.

There was a soft knock at the door. "Libby? Can I come in, please?" Mel's voice was as broken as mine.

I nodded. Zane got up and let Mel in, leaving us alone.

She looked as bad as I felt. "Fuck I'm so sorry, I should have told you before. At the baby shower, Olivia, she saw your ultrasound, you know, they have your name on it. She knew you and Richard were together, so she put two and two together and realised it was his baby. She promised she wouldn't tell him, but you have to tell him yourself." She placed a hand on my belly. "And soon. Don't leave it too long, he's already missed out on a lot with you. He loves you, so much."

"He's married to her though, what if they want to take custody of the baby once its born?"

"No, he's not. They were separated, and their divorce came through last week. They wouldn't dream of taking your baby away from you. They aren't that kind of people, Libs."

"Then why is she here?"

"That's something you'll have to ask her, but for now, I think we both need to rest. You've had a bad trot over the last few days old girl, we don't need you to have that baby early."

I nodded and settled down on the bed. Zane came back in and put my clothes back.

****

Bed rest totally sucked, though I did sneak down to the kitchen a few times and helped peel potatoes for dinner, until Zane ushered me back with the clucking of his tongue like a disgruntled matron. He could see how utterly bored I was, so he brought up baby and House and Garden magazines, hoping I'd find ideas for the nursery.

I couldn't wait to move into our new house—I picked neutral colours, lemons and pastel greens. I still hadn't asked the baby's sex, even though the ultrasound technician could easily tell what it was by this point. I didn't want to know, after all, if it was a girl, I'd have some lovely new furniture from Zane for my little princess to

231

enjoy. Otherwise, Aunty Zee would be getting an expensive bottle of cognac.

We'd also heard that Lisa was going to pull through, though it would be some time before she would be able to return to work, for that, I was thankful.

****

I relaxed in a garden lounge watching Aaron playing in the garden. The little bugger was growing so fast and was crawling on chubby hands and knees. I looked forward to a similar scene about a year from now, watching as my own child played in our garden.

Mel came over with a glass of juice in each hand, passing me one, while the boys set up the portable marquee for Mel's birthday bash. I'd been having a few twinges in my back recently, and was having more trouble sleeping, though I was now at the thirtieth week, the time seemed to be ticking by fast. Mel was due two weeks before me, and was bigger.

We took our 'supervisor' roles very seriously, cajoling and teasing the men as they set up the marquee, and trestle tables. Caterers from London were arriving and setting up. Mel's party was going to be a nice affair, but I felt exhausted and my back ached terribly. "I'm going to go lay down for a while," I said.

Mel nodded. "Okay, I'll send someone up to check on you later."

I nodded as I headed back inside, waddling slowly up the stairs to my room where I collapsed onto the bed and snuggled up to a pillow, supporting my body against its fluffiness.

I woke to a kiss on my cheek and a scent that was familiar to me. "Hmm?" I murmured.

"Libby." Richard's voice came to me in the dark.

"What?" I sat up, just as a searing pain ripped through my belly.

"Oh fuck…" I whimpered, clutching my belly.

"Are you all right, Libby? Why is the bed all wet?" Richard's voice sounded a little panicked.

"Wet?" I asked, looking down. Sure enough, the bed and my dress were soaked.

"Oh shite… It's too early."

"Too early?" Richard asked, looking confused.

"Richard, my water broke. I'm having our baby."

He paled. "It's coming now?" he asked.

"I nodded, wincing as another contraction bit into me.

"What the fuck?!"

Chapter Forty-Two.

"Oh my god, oh my god, oh my god!" Zane chanted as Richard held my hand in the back seat of Mel's Range Rover. Robbie drove like a maniac to the hospital where I was whisked away to a delivery room.

"Richard! I want Richard and Zane!" I begged, I was terrified for my baby.

"Who is the father, honey?" a nurse asked.

"Richard, but I want Zane here too. He's my support person." I moaned as another contraction hit. "It's too fucking early, way too fucking early," I cried.

A nurse came and dabbed my tears. Two panicking males burst through the door, surgical masks and gowns covering them as they ran to my side. Richard on one, Zane taking the other as I huffed and moaned with each contraction getting closer and closer.

"How far along are you honey?"

"Just at thirty weeks," I panted.

"She has preeclampsia," Zane said. "She was in the hospital for it only last week."

The nurse nodded. "Well it looks like this little one wants to come early."

She moved aside for the doctor to examine me.

"You're just about ready Miss Hastings," he said. He turned to the nurse. "Have the NICU ready."

"Yes doctor." The nurse moved out of my line of sight, but I could hear everything happening, the beeping of the heart monitor they'd hooked me up to, Richard's fast breathing, the way he gripped my hand.

"Richard." I panted. "I'm sorry I didn't tell you before… I was so afraid."

"I know, it's all right. We have a second chance here Libby. If you want to take it, I'll be here for you, and our baby." He pulled his mask down and kissed my hand. I gripped his fingers tight as another contraction hit, it was a big one.

"Okay, Miss Hastings, I think we're ready to bring this little one into the world. On the next one, I need you to push."

He looked up over my splayed legs. I nodded. I felt it hit me like a fucking Mack truck. I squeezed Richard's fingers and cried out as I pushed, sweat beading on my forehead as I worked to bring my baby into the world. Another two more pushes and I heard the mewling of our son.

"Oh… My god…" Zane whimpered before he collapsed into a dead faint on the delivery room floor.

"Looks like we have a fainter," the doctor chuckled. "Hey mum and dad, here's your baby boy."

They placed him gently on my chest before they whisked him away to the NICU.

Richard looked at me, tears shining in his eyes. "Libs, he's beautiful, he's perfect, he's ours." He leaned forward, and kissed me, his lips so tender and filled with love that I began to weep. I raised my hand and pulled him closer against me.

"I'm sorry," I sobbed.

"Shh, it's all right, we have a lot to talk about," he promised, leaning back and wiping my eyes.

"Huh? What happened?" Zane asked groggily as a nurse waved something under his nose to rouse him.

"You fainted, you pillock," I chuckled.

"Really? Damn. What was it?"

"A bottle of cognac."

"Woohoo!" Zane cheered.

"A bottle of cognac?" Richard asked, confused.

"Zane and I had a bet, if it was a girl he'd buy the furniture for the nursery and put it together, if it was a boy, I'd buy him a bottle of cognac."

The doctors finished up with me cleaning me and checking me over for any issues from the preeclampsia, which I was assured would clear up now I've had the baby, and I was wheeled out to the maternity ward.

"When can I see him again?" I asked. Richard walked beside me, his hand clasped with mine

"We'll have him in there for a little while, until we know he's grown a little bit more, a few weeks, more depending on if there's any complications."

Richard nodded. I felt my heart rate spike. "Complications?"

"Your son is premature, but hopefully he'll be fine. He might have a few little things that might crop up here or there, but neonatal medicine has come a long way," the nurse said as the orderlies helped me into bed. "Now, we want you to rest."

I nodded and closed my eyes. Richard lay his head down on the bed beside me, and I rested my fingers over his hair, stroking softly until I drifted off from exhaustion.

I woke up alone.

"Richard?" I called softly, trying to not disturb the other sleeping mothers.

A nurse looked up from the nurses' station across from my room. She came in and smiled. "You're looking for your husband? He's with your son in the NICU. Did you want to go visit him too?"

I nodded, eager to get to my boy. The nurse helped me out of bed and into a wheelchair. She called for an orderly who wheeled me down to the NICU, where Richard was sitting beside a clear plastic crib, a hand inside the ports, and our son clutching a finger.

The orderly wheeled me in.

"Hey," I said, looking in on our baby.

His red wrinkled skin made him look like a miniature old man who had spent too many days out in the sun. He had a small tube in his nose, affixed with a clear tape to his tiny cheek. He looked so small, so fragile

"This is a gift, Libs, you can't understand how precious this is to me," he said, softly, with tears in his eyes.

"I'm so sorry I didn't tell you."

"I understand, you were afraid. Mel told me you saw Olivia and I going to a jewellery store." He sniffed.

"I did. I saw you hug and kiss her, and I know she called you a few times."

"We were going through a separation and divorce. I wasn't there for her when she needed me." He paused, as if trying to find the courage to say what he had to, to help me to understand.

"We had a daughter, her name was Daisy. She was beautiful, but she died when she was two months old. She died from SIDS." He wiped his eyed again, keeping his gaze on our son. "After the funeral, I lost myself in work, never thinking on how it affected her, only caring about my next big job, the next arrest. I came home one night to find dinner on the table, and her things all gone. She left me, and I deserved it."

What. The. Fuck?

Chapter Forty-Three.

"You didn't deserve that, you were both grieving in your own way."

"We went our separate ways, and she filed for divorce. Then, shortly after I'd met you she called me, asking for help. She'd wanted to find a nice little place to set up as a Bed and Breakfast. It was always one of her dreams. I owed her for being a shitty husband, and she had no-one else to turn to. Her parents were both dead and she was an only child. So, I helped her. Gave her a place to stay while we looked at properties, and then your old cottage came up, and it was perfect, I know this because, well, I'd helped clean it up, remember?"

I nodded, remembering I watched the sweat glistening off his muscular arms, and wanting to find a nice, private, shady thicket and have my wicked way with him.

"Then we were lucky enough to get it at auction. It went for a good price too, even if I say so myself. After you left, I worked on helping Liv get the bed and breakfast set up, fixing the cottage, doing the gardens. You wouldn't recognise it now. Mel kept me up to date with you in LA, and I can't tell you how many times I wanted to jump on a plane and come see you, to try to get you to come back so we can work things out." He looked at me, eyes hopeful. "Tell me, please, Libs, is there still a chance for us? Even if there's not, I still want to be part of his life."

I took his free hand, not wanting him to lose the connection to our boy. "Yes, Richard, I never stopped feeling for you, thinking of you even when I felt like you'd ripped my heart in two. It still was, and always will be all for you, even if you were a bit of a dick to start with."

He chuckled. "I know, and, well, I was just doing my job."

We were distracted by a soft knocking at the doorjamb. A nurse stood there with a soft smile on her face.

"Sorry to interrupt, but would you like to hold your son?"

"Abso-fucking-loutly." I smiled, Richard gently pulled his finger free of the baby's grasp and pulled free from the crib.

The nurse took our boy out and gently picked him up, cradling him a moment before she settled him into my waiting arms.

"Oh my god, he's so beautiful."

"We had to put a nasal-gastric tube in, so we could feed him." The nurse explained. "He'll be ready for a change of nappy soon, did Daddy want to do that?" she asked Richard.

"I've already done one." He said with pride.

"What? When?"

"While you were asleep, he needed a nappy change."

"You've been here with him all this time?" I asked, my heart melting.

"Between you and him, yes." He looked down at the little one I my arms. "Have you thought of any names yet?"

"Nope." I shook my head. "I didn't even know the sex until he came along."

"I'm sure we'll think of something soon." Richard smiled. A few hours later, we left our boy back at the NICU and returned to my room.

We had visitors. A room full of flowers and balloons had materialised. Zane was sitting in one of the two chairs, sipping coffee while Mel sat in the other. Adam, with little Aaron, Robbie, Mrs Whittaker, and Mr Whittaker in his wheelchair, even Olivia, were all settled in my small room, the women perched on the bed.

"What's this, a bloody mother's conference?" I asked.

"That's one," Mel said, dropping a pound into a new jar before she handed it to me.

"What's this?" I asked.

"Well, you never let me give it to you at the baby shower, so this is as good a time as any." She smirked. I looked at the jar, in glittery letters, the label read 'Libby's Swear Jar'.

"Oh, come on, I don't swear that much!" I protested good naturedly.

"Honey, you swear more than a sailor on payday. That baby boy in there? You know what his first words will be? It's going to be Fu-." Zane said.

243

He stopped as I held the jar out to him, shaking it so the one pound rattled against the glass.

He poked his tongue out at me. I flipped him the bird. I turned to Olivia.

"I need to apologise to you for my behaviour."

"No, you don't," she said.

I shook my head. "Yes, I do. I wasn't aware that you and Richard weren't together anymore. I've had bad experiences in the past, where I've been the 'other woman' and hadn't realised it. I've treated you badly, based on a misconception, and I apologise."

"Libby, I don't want you to stress over it, it's fine. Richard should have told you before what was going on. I'm surprised he didn't. But I can understand, maybe he was afraid of what you might think, might do. We were both hurt before, by each other after we lost Daisy."

I stopped her. "He told me about that, I'm so sorry."

"Thank you, she's still part of us. I hope one day, Richard will tell her brother about her."

"I'll make sure he does, and besides, you're still part of the family, right?"

She looked at Richard, slightly confused.

"I'm not sure, I don't know what you mean."

"Well, I'd like you to be." I turned to Richard. "If that's fine with Richard?"

"Of course, Olivia, you'll always be part of the family."

She smiled. "Thank you, both so much." She hugged me, and then Richard. "Well, I'd best be off, I have some guests arriving tonight and I need to finish getting their room ready."

She said her goodbyes and left. I turned my attention to Mel.

"Did I ruin your party?" I asked her.

"No, actually, it was winding down when Richard came screaming down the stairs calling for help." She giggled. "How is he? Do you have pictures? A name?"

"Oh, no, I didn't get any pictures of him." I said, realising that I had done nothing of the sort.

"That's okay, I got a few." Richard smiled. "He's perfect, they think he'll be in there a few weeks until he's strong enough for the outside world, but with a mum like Libby, he'll be out sooner," he said, passing his phone around to show them the pictures of the baby.

Zane scooted off his seat and came to sit next to me on the bed. "When we get home, I got a surprise for you."

"Oh god," I said, knowing what some of Zane's surprises were like.

"You'll love it, I promise."

"Oh, now that makes me *really* scared to see it."

"Trust me." He winked.

'*Trust me*'

Really, Zane?

What The fuck?!

Chapter Forty-Four.

We left the hospital a month later with baby Andrew safe and secure in his carrier. Richard had spent almost every day at my bedside or at little Andy's while we changed and fed him. His nasal-gastric tube had been removed and he was still getting used to being breastfed, though the doctors were pleased with his progress and deemed him fit and well enough to go home, as long as we ensured we made weekly visits to his paediatrician and the maternity nurse to make sure he was growing enough.

Richard drove past the turn off that left town and would take us to Mel's place.

"Uh, you missed the turn," I said to him.

He smiled, taking my hand in his. He brought it to his lips and kissed it gently. We'd grown closer again since being reunited, and I felt the love beating in my heart every time I looked at him, and our son.

"No, I didn't." He smirked.

"Yes, you did, this isn't the way home."

"Oh, yes, it is." I shook my head in exasperation.

He turned another corner and pulled into a driveway. The house was familiar, then I realised, it was the house Zane had bought. "Oh crap, the cognac!" I had completely forgotten about it.

"I got you covered love." Richard leaned back and pulled a brown paper bag out from behind the front passenger seat.

He got out of the car and, like the gentleman he was, opened my side for me and helped me out. I moved to the back door, juggling my purse, the baby's nappy bag and the bottle of cognac in my arms.

"I'll get Andy out." He smiled, leaving me to right myself with my armloads.

With everyone and everything unloaded from the car, we made our way to the front door Zane opened it as we hit the first step.

"Welcome home, you two." Zane smiled, handing Richard the keys.

"Wait, what?"

"Zane has given us this house."

"Uh… He what?"

"It's yours sweetheart, my gift to both of you, well all three of you." He leaned down and grinned at Andy, who was fast asleep.

"Zane, you can't just do that."

"Yes, I can."

"No, you can't."

"Libby, shut the fuck up and take the damned keys," he said crossing his arms.

"Fine, take your damned cognac," I said poking my tongue out.

"Very nice." Zane grinned, checking the bottle over. "Good price, a house for a bottle of cognac." Richard chuckled. "Come, I want to show you the nursery."

We followed him through the house, past the kitchen and towards the back hallway where there was a row of doors, all closed.

"Bathroom is in there," Zane said, pointing to a door in the middle. "Mommy and Daddy's room here." He pointed to the door on the right of the bathroom, and opposite that, was another room. "Mommy, won't you do the honours?" Zane asked, taking my armful of crap.

I gripped the handle and opened the door. I gasped. Oh my god, Zane, this is… It's gorgeous."

The nursery was fully furnished, a beautiful wooden crib waited for Andy to sleep in, a change table and rocking chair and tallboy sat in prime positions around the room. The walls were painted a soft robins-egg blue, and lacey curtains and a pull-down blind with a rocking horse motif adorned the windows. I wandered deeper into the room, looking over the mass of stuffed toys sitting in the corner. I looked over the tallboy, pulling open drawers and seeing the clothes inside. I turned around and saw Richard on one knee, a white box in his hand, open to show a beautiful diamond ring inside.

"Libby, I want to spend the rest of my life with you, will you do me the honour of becoming my wife?"

I felt the tears in my eyes break free as I stepped to him. we'd come a very long way, through love, hurt, separation and our beautiful miracle that brought us back together again. I wanted everything he had to offer me, and I was willing to give him everything else in return. I took his hands in mine and looked into his eyes.

What the fuck?

"YES!"

THE END.

Other books by Scarlett J Rose:

Independent books:

The FML Series:

FML

WTF

OMG *(Coming soon!)*

Redemption of the Fallen Series.

Demon's Embrace

Angel's Redemption

Demon's Bargain *(Coming Soon!)*

Maelstrom MC.

Firestorm.

Broken Flowers:

Desert Rose

Evernight Publishing:

The Trenin Alliance:

Subject 26-A

(2017 Evernight Publishing Reader's choice runner up in Science-fiction Category)

Fallen Star

Romance on the Go Standalones.

Guarding Her

The Indecent Proposal of Mrs Cortez

More to come!

'Like' Scarlett J Rose on Facebook for upcoming releases and more information!

www.facebook.com/scarlettjrose/

www.ingramcontent.com/pod-product-compliance
Lightning Source LLC
Chambersburg PA
CBHW071514110726

47908CB00003B/840